Conten

D0404841

Introduction   v

Chapter 1   The Man with no Memory   1

Chapter 2   Names and Addresses   6

Chapter 3   Trained to Kill   14

Chapter 4   Following the Money   22

Chapter 5   The Man is Cain   30

Chapter 6   Messages   38

Chapter 7   Treadstone Seventy-one   43

Chapter 8   At Home with the General   49

Chapter 9   Trouble at Les Classiques   54

Chapter 10   Friends or Enemies?   61

Chapter 11   Rebirth   65

Activities   71

Contents

The Bourne Identity

ROBERT LUDLUM

Level 4

Retold by Andy Hopkins and Jocelyn Potter
Series Editors: Andy Hopkins and Jocelyn Potter

Pearson Education Limited
Edinburgh Gate, Harlow,
Essex CM20 2JE, England
and Associated Companies throughout the world.

ISBN: 978-1-4082-2108-2

This edition first published by Pearson Education Ltd 2010

3 5 7 9 10 8 6 4 2

Original text copyright © Robert Ludlum, 1980
This edition arranged with the Orion Publishing Group Ltd, London
Text copyright © Pearson Education Ltd 2010
Illustrations by Chris King

Set in 11/14pt Bembo
Printed in China
SWTC/02

Published by Pearson Education Limited in association with
Penguin Books Ltd, and both companies being subsidiaries of Pearson PLC

For a complete list of the titles available in the Penguin Readers series please write to your local
Pearson Longman office or to: Penguin Readers Marketing Department, Pearson Education,
Edinburgh Gate, Harlow, Essex CM20 2JE, England.

Introduction

*It happened so quickly that there was no time to think. A man walked
into him and then his eyes widened in disbelief.*

"No! My God! It cannot ... You're dead!"

*The patient's hand seized his shoulder. "I lived. What do you
know?"*

When Dr. Washburn's patient is pulled from the waters of the
Mediterranean, he has been shot many times and is close to
death. The doctor discovers that the man's face has been changed
and that he has lost his memory—maybe forever. Who is the
patient? *What* is he? And what was he before the attack in which
he almost lost his life?

The patient himself has no idea who he is. He has knowledge
and skills, but they are not the knowledge and skills of an
ordinary man. Why is he so comfortable with guns? Why is
the number of a bank account recorded on a small piece of film
which was hidden under his skin? Why does he know so much
about important world events but not his own name?

As he begins the search for his identity, the patient is seriously
worried. He soon realizes that a lot of people are glad that he is
dead. Then, when they learn that he is alive, they want to kill
him. But why? What is hidden in the patient's past? And does
he have a future?

The Bourne Identity is one of a number of very popular stories
about the man who has lost his memory. *The Bourne Identity*, *The
Bourne Supremacy*, and *The Bourne Ultimatum* are all bestselling
books which have also been made into successful movies starring
Matt Damon.

The movie stories are different in many ways, though, from

the stories of the books that they come from. The main character in the movie of *The Bourne Identity*, for example, has a different level of responsibility for the world of killing that he lives in. The story of Carlos the Jackal is also very important in Ludlum's book, but was removed for the film.

In this book, Carlos is one of many people and organizations who would like the hero to be dead. His character here is Ludlum's invention, but a real assassin called Carlos the Jackal—the Venezuelan-born terrorist Ilich Ramirez Sanchez, described in the newspaper report at the beginning of this book—is in fact now being punished for his crimes in a French prison.

This use of real but fictionalized people and of actual events in international politics is typical of Ludlum's writing, and it is one of the qualities that makes his stories so exciting. Against the background of big events, his heroes must fight against powerful national and international organizations, often governmental and financial. Terrorists are usually the tools of these organizations, employed for their skills as killers—they are not people with strong political or personal beliefs.

Ludlum's heroes are lonely and confused. They do not know who their true friends are or who their enemies might be. The action moves from country to country. It is often violent and always very fast. From the first page, the reader wants to know more. Millions of readers have discovered that it is very difficult to put a Robert Ludlum book down before the end.

Robert Ludlum, the writer of *The Bourne Identity*, was born in New York City in 1927 and grew up in New Jersey. He enjoyed acting and football at school, but became a soldier in 1945 before going to college. He then worked as an actor on stage and on television, and he produced many stage plays. This experience of theater, he said in later interviews, taught him how to keep the interest of his readers.

Ludlum's first book, *The Scarlatti Inheritance*, appeared in 1971, and it became an immediate bestseller. During World War 2, officials in Washington hear that a top Nazi commander is prepared to share secrets which will shorten the war—but at the same time, equally secret information about the Scarlatti inheritance will become known and will destroy many Western public figures. Ludlum's next book, *The Osterman Weekend* (1973), was made into a movie. In the story, a news show host is told by a CIA officer that some of his friends are a danger to the nation and the world—but which of them are really enemies and which are true friends?

From the mid-1970s, Ludlum was a very successful full-time writer. He and his family moved from New Jersey to a farmhouse in Long Island, and had a second home in Florida.

Robert Ludlum died in 2001, but other books have appeared in his name since then, including more *Bourne* books. Some of these were written or part-written by Ludlum; others are similar works by other writers. Ludlum did not want his name to be forgotten after his death.

It was not likely that he would be forgotten, though. More than 200 million copies of his books have been sold, and there have been translations into thirty-two languages. Robert Ludlum's exciting stories are admired and enjoyed by readers around the world.

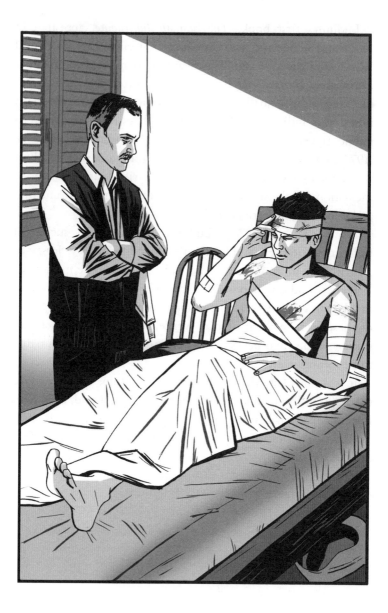

"My name is Geoffrey Washburn. What's yours?"
"I don't know," he said.

Chapter 1 The Man with no Memory

"Who's there? Who's in this room?"

Washburn went quietly to the bed. He did not want to make a sudden noise or movement that could cause his patient new psychological damage. The next few minutes would be as important as the surgery that he had performed on the man many times during the past month.

"A friend," he said softly. "You speak English. I thought you would. How do you feel?"

"I'm not sure."

"You were brought here, to the French island of Ile de Port Noir, by fishermen who found you in the Mediterranean. You'd been shot, many times. I'm a doctor—*your* doctor. My name is Geoffrey Washburn. What's yours?"

The stranger was silent for a minute. Then he turned and looked into the doctor's eyes. "I don't know," he said.

Weeks passed.

"It will take time. Don't fight it."

"You're drunk," his patient said.

"I usually am," Washburn agreed. "That's why I lost my job

1

in a London hospital and came here. But I'm a good doctor, and I saved your life. I've watched you, and I've listened to you. You speak English, French, and an Asian language—I don't know which one. You've been violent—at times I've had to tie you to the bed to protect your wounds. And your face really interests me."

"Tell me."

"It's been changed. You've had surgery to every part of it—eyes, nose, chin. And your hair is not your natural color."

The stranger thought about this. "But why?" he said.

"Think! What are you? What *were* you?"

"An international salesman? A teacher of languages?"

"No," said Washburn. "Your body is strong. Your hands are strong. But you're not a builder or a fisherman—you have a good mind and wide knowledge. When you were unconscious, you talked of places that I've never heard of."

"What else have you learned about me?"

"I had to be sure that your mind was strong enough to accept this." Washburn held up a small square of plastic. "I found this piece of film under your skin. It says: *Die Bank Gemeinschaft, 11 Bahnhofstrasse, Zurich. 07-1712-0-14-260.*"

"Bank details?"

"Exactly. The numbers are in your handwriting—they're your signature for an account at a bank in Zurich."

More time passed.

"There are no rules," the doctor told him. "Amnesia can be physical—from a head wound—or psychological. I think, for you, it's both. Your mind is protecting itself. But we're making progress. We're finding out what you do best." He opened a closet and took out a gun. "Take this to pieces." He threw it to the other man.

The patient looked at the gun. Then his fingers started moving, and in seconds the gun was in pieces.

"You see? You have experience—a lot of experience—of guns. You're a professional, but not, I believe, a soldier. I'm thinking of the surgery to your face. Your skills, and your normal behavior, will slowly come back to you. But your physical brain is not what it was. I don't know if it will ever connect those skills with your past. Your memories have been destroyed."

The man sat silently. Then he said, "The answer's in Zurich."

"Yes, you're strong enough now. I've made arrangements. There's a boat here from Marseilles. The captain will leave you on a beach outside the city."

The man with no memory looked at him. "So it's time."

"It's time. I know what you're feeling. A sense of helplessness because until now I've been your guide. But you're *not* helpless, believe me. You *will* find your way."

"To Zurich."

"To Zurich," agreed the doctor. "Here—take this. Two thousand francs*—all that I have. And my passport. We're about the same age, and it's eight years old. People change."

"What will *you* do?"

"I won't need it if I don't hear from you. If I do, you'll help me leave here—not just with money, but in ways you can't imagine."

"You're a good man."

"I think *you* are, too—as I've known you. I didn't know you before. I can't judge the man you were."

♦

There were no lights on the French coast. The captain pointed to a small beach.

"We can't go closer. You'll have to swim from here."

---

* francs: old French money, used before the change to euros; at that time the value of 2,000 francs was about 500 American dollars. Swiss francs are still used in Switzerland.

"Thank you for helping me."

"Don't thank me. When you were brought in from the storm, three of my men were also hurt, on my boat. The doctor helped them. I had no fish, so no money. You're my payment."

"I need papers," the man said, sensing that more help was possible. "I need a passport to be changed."

The captain was silent. Then he said, "I'll be in a café in Marseilles this evening, Le Bouc de Mer. You'll need money for the papers."

"How much?"

"That's a matter for the man you'll speak to there. A lot."

The patient thought about the money from the doctor. It wouldn't be enough. "I'll be there," he said.

Some time later, he walked through the narrow streets of the small coastal town. Money. He found the richest area.

In a store, he heard a conversation between the owner and a customer.

"Where's the Marquis* today?"

"Drunk, in the apartment above the café next door. Waiting for a woman. I had to drive him from the house without his wife seeing him. I've left his car here, but he won't be able to drive it. I'll come back later."

The patient walked around the next-door building, looking through doors and windows and wondering which car belonged to the Marquis.

A woman arrived—an attractive woman in a very short skirt—and soon he saw her at an upstairs window. The patient went inside, took the stairs to the first floor and, in one quick movement, broke the door down.

"*Nom de Dieu*† !" The man on the bed looked up in shock. "Did my wife hire you? I'll pay you more!"

---

* Marquis: the title of an upper-class man in France
† *Nom de Dieu!: In God's name!*, French words spoken in surprise

"Keep quiet," said the patient, "and you won't get hurt."

He quickly put on the Marquis's expensive clothes and took his money, watch, and car keys.

"Please leave me *your* clothes," the Marquis cried.

"I'm sorry. I can't do that." He picked up his own and the woman's clothes. Then he noticed a telephone on a desk by the window and pulled the wire from the wall.

"The police will find you," the Marquis said angrily.

"I don't think you'll report a crime. How will you explain it to your wife?"

You're not helpless. You will find your way. What kind of past produced the skills that were returning to him now?

He had difficulty with the controls in the Marquis's Jaguar. He had, he thought, no past experience with cars like this. He followed the signs to Marseilles, and found a garage selling new and used expensive cars. Ten minutes later, he had exchanged the car for six thousand francs—about a fifth of its value, but no questions asked. Soon after that, he had sold the watch and bought clothes and a soft leather suitcase. Then he found a hotel and rested until it was time for his appointment at Le Bouc de Mer.

The patient made his way through the crowded tables of the café until he found the captain. There was another man at the table, thin and pale-faced with narrow eyes.

"How much to change this passport—by ten o'clock tomorrow?"

"Three and a half thousand francs. And I'll need a photo."

"I had one done on the way here." The patient passed it to him.

A meeting was arranged for the next day, and the captain was given five hundred francs under the table. Then the patient walked toward the door.

It happened so quickly that there was no time to think. A man walked into him and then his eyes widened in disbelief.

"*No!* My God! It cannot … You're *dead*!"

The patient's hand seized his shoulder. "I lived. What do you *know*?"

The other man's face was red and angry. He pulled out a knife. "I'll finish it now," he said.

The man with no memory brought his other hand down, hard, and kicked with all his strength. His attacker fell back and the knife was seen by the people around them.

"Take your argument outside, or we'll call the police!"

The patient could not move in the crowd. His attacker ran, holding his stomach, out into the darkness of the street.

He thought I was dead—wanted *me to be dead. And now he knows I'm alive.*

Chapter 2 Names and Addresses

He knew the name of the hotel. Carillon du Lac. He had given it to the taxi driver without thinking. He knew the reception area, and the big glass windows that looked out over Lake Zurich. He had been there before.

"It's good to see you again, sir," the receptionist said.

But I don't know you! I don't know me*! Help me! Please!*

"Thank you," he said. "I've hurt my hand. Could you fill in the form for me and then I'll try to sign it." The patient held his breath.

"Of course, sir." The receptionist completed the form, then turned it around for the signature.

Mr J. Bourne, New York, N.Y., U.S.A.

He stared at it. He had a name—part of a name. *J. Bourne.* John? James? Joseph? He signed.

The receptionist bent forward. "The usual conditions, sir? You will be informed of any calls or visitors, but only calls from your company should be put straight through to your room.

Treadstone Seventy-one, if I remember correctly."

More information! Another name! He had a country, and a city, and a company that employed him—or that *had* employed him. And he was protected from unwanted visitors.

"That's correct. Thank you."

Upstairs in his room, he called the New York operator. Her words were quite clear. "We have no telephone number for a company of that name, sir."

He put the phone down. Might Treadstone Seventy-one be a code, a way of reaching Mr. J. Bourne of New York City? He left his room and walked into the street. His feet seemed to take him on a route that he knew—and then there was the Gemeinschaft Bank.

He entered through the heavy glass doors and was directed to a first floor receptionist.

"Your signature, please," the man requested, passing him a form.

He looked and understood; no name was needed this time, just the number of the account. He wrote out the numbers and was shown to a private room.

"The door will lock behind you," the receptionist told him. "It is usual for holders of special accounts to telephone before they come."

"I knew that," Washburn's patient lied, "but I'm in a hurry."

He walked inside, heard the door lock, sat down, and waited.

Finally another, metal door opened. A bank officer introduced himself as Herr★ Apfel and invited the visitor into his office. The "signature" was requested again, and within minutes the receptionist entered with a black metal container.

"May I unlock the box?" Herr Apfel asked.

"Please do—open it."

The banker looked shocked. "I said 'unlock,' not 'open.' Your

★ Herr: the German word for Mr.

7

identity might be listed, and I do not need to know it."

"But if I wanted the money to be sent to another bank?"

"Then a name would be needed."

"Open it."

The banker opened the box and passed the papers to the other man, who stared at the top page in disbelief. The amount in the account was 11,850,000 Swiss francs. More than 4 million American dollars. *How? Why?*

The bottom statement showed that the first payment into the account had been from Singapore: 5,175,000 Swiss francs. Below that was an envelope with "Owner only, officer of the Treadstone Seventy-one Company" typed on it. He opened it, and read:

Owner: Jason Charles Bourne

Address: Unlisted

Nationality: American

Jason. He felt a pain in his stomach, a ringing sound in his ears. *Why did he feel that he was falling into darkness again?*

When he returned to the reception area an hour later, after a meeting with another bank official, Herr Koenig, 3,000,000 Swiss francs had been sent to the Marseilles account of Dr. Geoffrey Washburn, who had saved his life. The money would cure or kill the alcoholic. Four million francs was on its way to a bank in Paris, for the use of Jason C. Bourne. Another 100,000 francs in large notes had been handed over by Herr Koenig in cash.

Herr Koenig walked with him to the elevator, past two men who were sitting at opposite ends of the room. Out of the corner of his eye, Bourne noticed movement. Koenig had turned to both of the men. One took a radio out of his pocket and spoke into it. The other took out a gun. The men moved toward Bourne, who was forced to back into the empty elevator.

As the elevator doors closed, with the gun at his head, Bourne moved suddenly to the right, then swept his foot off the floor and up to the man's arm, knocking the gun from his hand. His body continued to turn and his shoulder crashed into the other man's stomach, throwing him against the wall. The man fell to the floor, unconscious.

The man at Le Bouc de Mer, Bourne knew, had wasted no time sending his message to Zurich. *Kill him!* He seized the other killer by his neck. "How many? How many are waiting downstairs?" No answer. He pushed the man's face into the elevator wall, opened his coat, and found another gun. He pointed it. "How many?"

"Two. One by the elevators. One by the car outside."

"What *kind* of car?"

"A Peugeot. Brown."

The elevator doors opened and a man in a dark coat wearing gold glasses stepped forward, recognized the situation, and pointed a silenced gun at Bourne.

Bourne quickly pushed his prisoner out in front of him, protecting himself from the gun. Shots were fired, people screamed for the police. His prisoner fell to the floor. Bourne seized the nearest person, the receptionist, threw him into the path of the man with the gold glasses, and ran through the doors. Then he slowed down and walked calmly away, past the man in the Peugeot, before he turned and watched.

As the first police car arrived, the man in gold glasses talked to the driver of the Peugeot. Then, unexpectedly, he returned to the bank, joining the police who were racing inside.

The Peugeot left and an ambulance arrived. Bourne turned away. He had to get to his hotel, pack, and leave Zurich—leave Switzerland. For Paris. *Why* Paris? Inside the bank, there had seemed to be no question. He had to go to Paris. But *why*?

At the Carillon du Lac, Bourne packed quickly and then started down again. There were three other guests in the elevator—two men and a red-haired woman. French-speaking Canadians, Bourne realized, and clearly at the hotel for a conference. As he followed them to the reception desk, he noticed a sign on the wall:

Welcome to members of the Sixth World Economic Conference

The woman was now speaking English to the receptionist.

"Dr. St. Jacques?" the man checked, and passed her an envelope.

Bourne moved toward the entrance, then stopped. A brown Peugeot was parked in the street outside, and the man with gold glasses was climbing out of the car. From another door, a second man appeared, wearing a raincoat with pockets that were wide enough for powerful guns.

How? How had they found him? Then he remembered and he felt sick. It had seemed so innocent at the time.

"Are you enjoying your stay in Zurich?" Herr Apfel had asked.

"Very much. My room looks out onto the lake. Very peaceful."

How many hotels looked out onto the lake? Two? Three? The names of the hotels came into his mind—*from where?*

They had seen him. But did they think they could walk into a crowded hotel and simply kill him? Of course they did. With silencers on their guns and people all around him, they could easily escape before they were identified. What made them think he would not scream for the police? And then the answer was clear. They knew that Jason Bourne could not expect police protection. *Why?*

He turned and saw the red-haired woman, still reading her message. He looked back at the entrance. The killers were moving through the crowd toward him. Bourne walked quickly toward the woman, seized her by the arm, and pulled her away from the reception desk. As she looked up at him in surprise, he showed her the end of the gun in his pocket.

"I don't want to frighten you," he said quietly, "but I have no choice. Take me to your conference room."

Surprise had turned to shock. "You can't …"

"Yes, I can." Unseen by the people around them, he pushed the gun into her side. "Let's go."

"I don't want to frighten you, but I have no choice."

Pale and shaking, she led him quickly to a large hall where a man was giving a talk.

"I'll scream," the woman whispered.

"I'll shoot," he promised.

He pushed her across the back of the hall and down toward the front. Heads turned in their direction. The speaker paused and then came three sharp, sudden sounds. Shots! Then screams. Running now, Bourne pulled the woman toward a door at the back of the stage, and out.

They were in a car park. He heard a metallic sound, saw a slight movement. Another killer. How did they know where to find him? Radios again, of course. He moved quickly to one side, his shoulder crashing into the woman's stomach, sending her to the ground. Shots hit cars near them. He jumped up, gun in hand, and fired three shots before throwing himself down.

He heard a scream—and then nothing. He started to get up, but could not. Pain spread through his body, through all the places where his wounds had been.

He looked over at the woman, who was slowly getting to her feet. He could not let her go! He had to stop her! He slowly made his way across the ground toward her.

"Help me up!" he said, hearing the pain in his voice.

"You're joking!"

"This gun is aimed at your face, Doctor. Help me up."

When he, too, was on his feet, he pulled the dead driver from the car and ordered the woman to get behind the wheel.

"Drive!" he said, climbing into the passenger seat.

Where could he go? The killers had seen his suitcase. They would watch the stations and the airports. But he had money—a lot of money. And he had to get to Paris.

"I work for the Canadian government," the woman said quickly. "I'm an economist. They expect me to contact them tonight. If they don't hear from me, they'll call the police."

Bourne took her bag and looked through it. Keys, money, her passport: Dr. Marie St. Jacques. And the message that was given to her at reception. A message allowing her vacation time.

As they drove across Zurich, stopping only to leave the car and steal another one, Bourne was following a memory. A restaurant—he knew it was important. He knew the way, but what was it called? Drei Alpenhäuser—yes! He had to go there.

Even before they parked, he had noticed that she was too quiet, too obedient. When they came to a stop, her door crashed open. She was half-way out into the street before Bourne's arm shot out and seized the back of her dress, forcing her back into the car. He took her hair and pulled her head toward him.

"I won't do it again," she cried. "I promise I won't."

"You will," he said quietly, "but if you run away before I let you go, I'll have to kill you. I don't want to, but I'll have to."

"You say you'll let me go," she said. "When?"

"In an hour or two. When we're out of Zurich and I'm on my way to somewhere else. Now dry your eyes. We're going inside."

"What's in there?"

He looked at the wide brown eyes that were searching his. "I don't know," he replied.

He showed her the gun—a reminder—and they entered the bar.

He had seen the inside of the Drei Alpenhäuser before. He recognized the heavy wooden tables, the lighting, the sounds. He had come here in another life.

A waiter led them to a table, where they ordered a drink. Bourne looked around. And then he saw a face across the room—a large head above a fat body. Bourne did not know the face, which was showing fear and disbelief—but the face knew him.

The fat man walked uncomfortably over to their table.

"Why are you here?" he asked. "I did what I was told to do. I gave you the envelope. I told no one about you. Have *others* spoken? I saw the police offer of a reward for information about

13

you, but I did *nothing*. The police have not come to me. If they did—you know—others would follow. My wife, my children … I've said nothing—*done* nothing!"

"Has anyone else? Tell me. I'll know if you're lying."

"Chernak is the only contact of yours that I know. He passed me the envelope—you know that. But he wouldn't say anything."

"Where is he now?"

"Where he always is. In his apartment on Löwenstrasse."

"What number?"

"You're testing me!" The fat man stared at him in fear. "37."

"Yes, I'm testing you. Who gave the envelope to Chernak? What was in it?"

"I have no idea who gave it to him. In it? Money, I guess. A lot of money. Now please, let me go! Get out of here!"

"One more question," Bourne said. "What was the money for?"

The fat man was shaking now. "No one told me, but every day I read the newspapers. Six months ago, a man was killed."

Chapter 3 Trained to Kill

They followed directions to Löwenstrasse. Marie was silent now, holding the wheel tightly. Bourne watched her and understood.

A man was killed … Jason Bourne had been paid to kill. The police had offered a reward. *Others would follow.* How many people were looking for him? Who were they? When would this end?

"There's number 37," he said. "Stop the car!"

Marie looked at him with fear in her eyes. "I don't want to go in there with you. I heard what the man said in the restaurant. If I hear any more, you'll kill me."

Bourne pulled his aching body out of the car. "His words made no more sense to me than to you. Maybe less." He saw the confusion on her face. "Let's go."

He did not press the bell below Chernak's name—he pressed others until someone opened the door. He walked with difficulty up the stairs, holding Marie's arm, and on his orders she knocked and then called out to the man inside.

The door opened and there, in a wheelchair, was a man with no legs.

"You're crazy!" the man cried. "Get away from here!"

"I'm tired of hearing that," Bourne said, and pulled Marie inside.

She willingly obeyed his orders to go to a small, windowless bedroom, and then Bourne turned back to Chernak.

"You promised that our last piece of business would be the final one," Chernak shouted, white-faced. "This is too dangerous."

"The envelope that you passed to our friend at the Drei Alpenhäuser," Bourne said. "Who gave it to you?"

"A messenger, like all the others. I don't know. You were paid, so I know you accepted the job. Why are you here now?"

Because I have to know. Because I don't understand. Help me!

He suddenly noticed Chernak's hand moving toward a bag hanging from his chair. The hand came out quickly, pointing a gun, and before Bourne could reach his own, Chernak fired twice. Pain filled Bourne's head and shoulder as he dived to one side, then crashed his other shoulder into Chernak's wheelchair. The legless man fell helplessly to the floor.

"They'll pay for your corpse!" he screamed. "Carlos will pay! I'll see you in hell."

Bourne fired a bullet into the man's head.

A long, terrible cry came from the bedroom door. A woman's cry. Bourne could hardly think for the pain. He had to take her—what was her name?—and get out.

"My God, you killed him!" she screamed, as he pulled her out of the apartment. "A man with no …"

Inside the car, Bourne tried to stop the blood. The head

wound was only a cut, but he was feeling sick and faint from the pain in his shoulder. An address came to him. He could picture the doorway. "Steppdeckstrasse," he ordered weakly.

The car did not move. What was she doing? Marie knocked the gun from his hand, pushed his head against the car window, then jumped out and ran.

He could not stay in the car. He cleaned off the blood as well as he could, then got out. Somewhere there would be a taxi.

No questions were asked when Bourne rented a room in the house in Steppdeckstrasse, and a doctor was found who also asked nothing. The pain in his head and shoulder was real, but the psychological damage was great. He needed to rest.

As he lay on the bed, words came to him: *A man was killed ... You accepted the job ...* And then: *They'll pay for your corpse! Carlos will pay!*

He heard a sudden, sharp noise outside the room. There was someone on the stairs. Bourne jumped off his bed, seized his gun, and ran to the wall by the door. The door crashed open; he pushed it back, throwing all his weight at it, then pulled the door open and kicked up at the man's head. Then, taking the man by the hair, he pulled him inside. A gun fell to the floor.

Bourne closed the door and listened. No sounds outside. He looked down at the unconscious man. Was he a thief? A killer? *Police?* Had the owner of the Steppdeckstrasse house decided to earn the reward? He searched the man's pockets and found cards and licenses in different names. He was a killer, a professional. Someone had hired him. Who knew that Bourne was there? The woman? Had he spoken the address? He could not remember.

He took the papers, put the gun in his pocket, then tied the unconscious man to the bed. Then he walked quietly and painfully down the stairs. The next doorway, he guessed—and he was right. He turned toward it and fired, hitting the second man in the leg.

16

"Is there anyone else?" he asked, with his gun at the man's head.

"No. Only two of us. We were paid."

"Who by?"

"You know."

"A man named Carlos?"

"I will not answer. Kill me first."

"Give me your car keys."

The man tried to push Bourne away. Bourne brought the end of the gun down on his head, and took his gun and keys. He hoped he would be able to drive.

He found the car and tried one key after another. Which was it? Suddenly a powerful light burned his eyes.

"Get out!" It was the man with the gold glasses. Behind him, a woman was led toward the car.

"That's him," Marie St. Jacques said softly.

"So this is what you look like," the Swiss man said to Bourne. "We have had so many descriptions."

"I'm happy to help the police, but I'd like to make my statement now—whatever you need—and go back to the hotel, please," Marie said.

The Swiss man looked up, and a second, larger man seized her arm. She stared at them, and then at Bourne, suddenly realizing.

"Let her go back to Canada," Bourne said. "She works for the Canadian government. And you'll never see her again."

"She has seen *us*," the Swiss man said. "There are rules." He turned to the larger man. "Take her in the other car, to the Limmat."

Bourne froze. Marie's corpse was going to be thrown in the Limmat River. "Scream!" he shouted.

She tried, but her scream was cut off by a blow to her neck and she was pulled, unconscious, toward a small black car. As the car drove away, Bourne felt sick. It was his fault. He had killed her.

"You were at the bank," he said. "You know I have money. Why not take mine?"

"Money is only useful if you have time to enjoy it," the Swiss man said. "I wouldn't have five minutes." He took the gun from Bourne's pocket and brought it down hard on Bourne's hands.

"My fingers—they're broken!" Bourne screamed. But he had quickly covered his right hand with his left; his left hand was bloody and useless, but he could still move the fingers on his right hand.

Another gunman joined them in the car and, as they headed across the city, he searched Bourne's clothes roughly, taking the money and documents.

"My leg!" Bourne screamed, bending down and reaching quickly inside his sock for the gun that was hidden there.

"Watch him!" cried the Swiss man, who was driving, but it was too late. Bourne had fired twice at the killer beside him and the gun was now at the head of the driver.

"Stop the car!" he shouted, but the car went faster.

"I can get you out of Zurich," the man said. "Without me, you can't leave. There are police looking for you everywhere. I don't think you want the police. Or I can crash the car and kill us both. I have nothing to lose."

"We'll talk," Bourne lied. "Slow down."

"Drop your gun on the seat next to me."

Bourne dropped his gun and the car slowed. Thirty kilometers an hour, eighteen, nine … He seized the man by the neck, then lifted his bloody left hand and spread the blood across the Swiss man's eyes. Reaching across with his right hand, he turned the wheel to the right, into a pile of garbage. He took the gun from the seat and fired. A dark-red hole appeared in the killer's head.

In the street, people were running toward the car. Bourne climbed into the front, pushed the corpse out, and drove away.

The Limmat. Marie would be killed in a dark, empty place near the water—or she already had been. He had to know. He could not walk away. He drove and searched, the length of the river, trying to forget the pain in his hand, the pain in his shoulder. He

Reaching across with his right hand, he turned the wheel to the right.

stopped only to push out the body from the back seat. Then, in an unlit parking area, he noticed the small black car. He stopped fifty meters away and opened his door. He heard a cry, low and frightened, from inside the car, the sound of a hand across a face, and another cry. Gun in hand, he walked slowly toward Marie and her assassin. The man was pulling off her clothes.

Filled with anger, but unable to shoot without hitting her, he broke the car window with his shoe.

"Stay inside!" he shouted to Marie, as the killer threw himself out of the car and onto the ground.

The killer fired and missed. Bourne fired and heard a cry. He had wounded the man—but not killed him.

"Who is it? What is happening?" An old man was shouting in German, holding a light in front of his face.

The killer ran to the old man and stood behind him, pulling him back. There was a shot, then the sound of running footsteps. The old man had served his purpose and was dead.

Bourne lowered himself to the ground. He could do nothing more. He did not care. Marie climbed slowly out of the car, shock in her eyes, holding her clothes to her body.

"Take the keys," he shouted. "Get out of here. Go to the police—real ones, with uniforms, this time."

"You saved my life," she whispered. "You were free, but you came back for me and saved my life."

He heard her through his pain. He felt her tying her clothes around his bleeding wounds. Then her hands were on his arms, gently pulling him up. As she helped him into the car, he could feel himself falling, falling into unconsciousness.

♦

"Can you hear me?" Marie's voice asked. "You're hurt, quite badly, but a doctor has seen you and you don't need to go to the hospital. A week's rest will be enough."

"Where are we?"

"In a village called Lenzberg, twenty-five kilometers from Zurich."

"How ...?"

"I decided to help you. It's the most difficult decision that I've ever made. I sat and thought for half an hour, but I couldn't go to the police after you saved me."

"Even knowing what I am?"

"I only know what I've heard, and I've seen a different man."

"Aren't you afraid of me?" he asked. "Afraid of what I've done?"

"Of course I am, but you're very weak and I have your gun. Also, you have no clothes. I've thrown them all away."

Bourne laughed through his pain, remembering the Marquis.

"Who are you?" Marie asked.

"They say my name is Jason Bourne."

"They say? What does that mean?"

"My life began five months ago on a small island in the Mediterranean ..."

As she sat by his bed, he talked through the night until there was nothing more to say.

"My God!" Marie said softly. "You know so little about yourself. You must really be suffering."

"How can you think about my suffering after what I've done to you?" he answered.

"They're separate—independent of each other. Outside Chernak's apartment, you said something about the fat man's words making no more sense to you than to me. I thought you were crazy, but now I understand. Why didn't you tell me before that Chernak tried to kill you?"

"There wasn't time before, and it didn't matter."

"It mattered to me. I thought you killed a defenseless man. The man with the gold glasses—the one who told me that he was a policeman—said that you were a professional assassin who must be stopped. But you were running for your life—*are* running for your life—and you're not a killer."

Bourne took her hand. "But there were envelopes filled with money, which I accepted. There were millions of dollars in a bank account. And you've seen my skills." He stared at the ceiling, the pain returning. "Those are the facts, Marie. You should leave."

"You don't have facts," she said. "I'm not a fool, but your facts come from the mouths of killers. And that bank account can be inspected by a company called Treadstone Seventy-one. That doesn't sound like the employer of a hired killer. I don't know what I believe, but I do know that I was going to die and you came to save me. I believe in you. I think I want to help you."

Chapter 4 Following the Money

During the daylight hours, Marie arranged for clothes, meals, maps, and newspapers. She also drove the stolen car fifteen kilometres away and left it, returning by taxi. Bourne used the time for rest and exercise to strengthen his damaged body.

While they were together, they talked, shyly at first, with many pauses and silences. Looks passed between them, and quiet laughter, and slowly they began to feel comfortable with each other. Marie, Bourne learned, had first studied history, but had then realized that most of history was shaped by economic powers, and so her future as an economist was decided. Marie questioned Bourne, examining the little he knew, trying to explain the holes in his knowledge.

"When you read the newspapers," she asked, "what's familiar?"

"Almost everything—names, places, political relationships."

"And when you look at the maps I've bought?"

"In some cases, I picture buildings, hotels, streets, faces. But the faces have no names."

"Did you meet people? Are there faces in buildings, in hotels?"

"Streets," he said, without thinking. "Quiet places. Dark places."

"What did they talk about?"

"I don't know. There aren't any voices. There aren't any words."

"Treadstone. That's your company, isn't it?"

"It doesn't mean anything. I couldn't find it."

"It could be a part of a company that buys other businesses secretly. Maybe you were working for American financial interests."

"But the account—no money was *leaving* it. I was selling, not buying. And why would people be trying to kill me?"

"What comes into your mind when you think of money?" Marie asked.

Don't do this! Don't you understand? When I think of money, I think of killing.

"I don't know," Bourne said. "I'm tired. I want to sleep now."

"You're wrong, you know," she said. "I've seen that look in your eyes, seeing things that may or may not be there—afraid that they are."

"They have been," he replied. "Explain the Steppdeckstrasse. Explain a fat man at the Drei Alpenhäuser."

"I can't—but you can't either. Find out, Jason. Find out."

"Paris," he said.

"Yes, Paris." Marie stood up and walked across the room to him. Then she reached down and touched his face. "Thank you for my life," she whispered.

"Thank you for mine," he answered, and she climbed into the bed. He held her tight.

Days and nights passed.

"I'm going to Paris with you today," Marie told him early one morning. "I can do things for you that you can't do yourself. You don't know enough about money and financial organizations. I do. And I have a position with the Canadian government, so I can get information—and protection. But at the first sign of

23

violence, I'll leave. I don't want to become a problem for you."

There was a long silence. Finally, Bourne said, "Why are you doing this?"

"I believe in the man who almost died for me," she answered.

"I accept," he said, reaching for her. "I shouldn't, but I need that belief very badly."

"I want to contact Peter, a friend of mine," Marie said. "If there is a Treadstone Seventy-one in a big company somewhere, he'll find out. I'll phone from a payphone in Paris, and ask him to call me back."

"And if he finds it? Do I contact the company?"

"Yes, very carefully and through another person—me, if you like. They haven't contacted you in six months. All that money was left in Zurich, untouched. Have they walked away from you? Do they think you've become part of something illegal that would make them look guilty, too?"

"But whatever we learn about Treadstone," Bourne said, "men are still trying to kill me, and I don't know why. I have to know why someone named Carlos will pay for my corpse ..."

Marie stared at him in shock. "What did you just say?" she asked. "The name—Carlos?"

"That's right."

"In all this time, you've never talked about him."

Bourne looked at her, trying to remember. She was right—he hadn't. Why not? Had he tried to block the name from his mind? "Does Carlos mean something to you?"

"My God. You really don't know," Marie said, studying his eyes. "He's an assassin, a man who's been hunted for twenty years or more. He's believed to be responsible for killing between fifty and sixty people, mostly politicians and army officers. No one knows what he looks like, but it's said that he works from Paris."

Bourne felt a wave of coldness spread through his body.

After separate flights to Paris, they had an arrangement to

meet in a small hotel. First, though, Bourne visited the Sorbonne library.

I *read the newspapers. Six months ago, a man was killed.* Those were the words of the fat man in Zurich.

Bourne counted back six months and collected newspapers for the ten weeks before that. Then he fingered through them quickly, page by page. Nothing. He returned the newspapers and took the ones for four and five months ago. More turning of pages ... and then he found it.

AMBASSADEUR LELAND EST MORT A MARSEILLES!★

He felt an explosion of pain hitting him between the eyes. His breathing stopped as he stared at the name. Leland. He knew it; he could picture the face. He read. American Ambassador Leland had been killed by a single shot from a high-powered gun. He had been in France asking the French government not to sell fighter planes to Africa and the Middle East. It was believed that he had been killed as a warning; the buyers and sellers of death were unhappy with his visit. The assassin was without doubt paid a lot of money.

Bourne closed his eyes. How could he know what he knew if he was not that assassin in Marseilles? He could not meet Marie now. She had been wrong, and his worst fears were real. He looked at the date of the newspaper. Thursday, August 26. Something was wrong. Washburn had told him, again and again, trying to help him remember: You were brought to my door on the morning of Tuesday, August 24 ... He was not in Marseilles on the twenty-sixth; he had not killed Leland!

Filled with happiness, he looked at his watch. It was time to find Marie. To reach her and hold her and tell her that there was hope.

In the room of their small hotel, Marie changed Bourne's

★ Ambassadeur Leland est mort à Marseilles: French for "Ambassador Leland dies in Marseilles"

hair color from dark to fair and he put on thick brown glasses. They formed a plan, and then went to the bank where Bourne's money was now sitting.

Marie went inside while Bourne stayed outside at a payphone. He rang the bank's number and asked for Foreign Services. He gave his name, and the name of the bank in Zurich, and asked to speak to a bank official. He then explained to a Monsieur* d'Amacourt that he needed to know whether the millions of francs had reached the bank.

"I am afraid," d'Amacourt explained, "that I cannot give that kind of information to a stranger on the telephone. I suggest that you come to the bank. My office is on the ground floor."

Bourne agreed to be there in half an hour, then ended the conversation. Seconds later, the telephone rang.

"His name's d'Amacourt—ground floor office," he told Marie.

"I'll find it," she said.

She was soon standing near the office. Would it happen? Was she right?

It happened. There was sudden activity as d'Amacourt's secretary rushed into his office, returning seconds later to call a number and speak, reading from her notebook. Two minutes later, d'Amacourt appeared at his door, questioned the secretary and returned to his room, leaving the door open. Then another man arrived with a small black case and entered the room. A light appeared on the secretary's telephone. D'Amacourt was making a call. Jason Bourne's account had secret instructions with it. The phone call had been made.

From his position at the payphone, Bourne saw three men hurrying up the street to the bank—and one of them he had seen before. In Zurich.

Bourne phoned the bank again and explained that his plans

* Monsieur, Madame: the French words for Mr. or sir, and Mrs.

had changed. He had to go to the airport and fly to London. Monsieur d'Amacourt should keep the account information in his office; Bourne would visit him the following day.

At the end of the working day, Marie pointed out d'Amacourt as he left the bank, then returned to the hotel. Bourne followed the banker to the door of a café and pulled him inside.

"Jason Bourne," he introduced himself. "Your friends must be confused by now, racing around the airport and wondering if you've given them false information."

D'Amacourt looked at him with fear in his eyes. "I know nothing. I only followed the instructions on the account."

They sat down and Bourne ordered drinks. "Tell me," he said.

"The instructions came from the Gemeinschaft Bank. I could lose my job if I talk to you."

"You could lose your life if you don't," Bourne said. "Name your price."

"You decide what value the information has to you. Your money came with special instructions, to be opened by me when the account-holder came for money. The instructions said that a telephone number should be called. But if I tell you more, you must think of another person who told you this. The information cannot come from me."

"I know a man," Bourne said, "a criminal at the Gemeinschaft. His name is Koenig."

"I'll remember that." D'Amacourt wrote down a Paris telephone number. Then he added, "But there was another number before that—a number in New York. That had been cut out—only the area code was still there—and this one had been put in its place. How valuable are you finding my information?"

"The price could be five figures," Bourne told him.

"Then I shall continue. I spoke to a woman, who gave me no name. She told me only that you were a dangerous man and must be kept in my office until a man arrived. He needed to see

27

you. The man came and I told him that you had changed your plans. That's all. Who are you, Monsieur?"

"Someone who must pay you a lot of money," Bourne said thoughtfully. "So how, now, do *we* get *our* money?"

"There is a way—forms completed and your identity checked by a lawyer. I do not have the power to stop that. Of course, I would have to make the phone call, but maybe only after I had signed the other papers on my desk. I do know a suitable lawyer. He would cost 10,000 francs. I would want 50,000."

◆

"So the account in Zurich was opened with those special instructions," Marie said thoughtfully. "That would be illegal in many countries, but some private European banks allow it. You probably knew that the instructions were there."

"Put there by Treadstone Seventy-one," Bourne agreed. "But someone was paid to change the telephone number. Koenig."

"That's a crime that could bring him ten years in a Swiss prison. He was paid a lot of money."

"By Carlos," Bourne said. *Carlos ... Why? What am I to him?*

"I'll phone the Canadian embassy and ask about the Paris telephone number that d'Amacourt used," Marie said. "My friend Peter gave me the name of a man there, Dennis Corbelier."

She called. Then they left the hotel so Marie could use a payphone to call Peter for information about Treadstone.

She came away from the phone, white and shaking.

Bourne took her in his arms. "What's wrong?"

"I spoke to his boss," Marie said faintly. "Peter's dead! He had phone calls from Washington D.C. and New York. Then he went to meet someone at the airport. On the way, he was shot in the throat! Peter! Oh, what have I done?"

"*You* have done nothing." Bourne could hardly breathe. "A bullet in the throat ... It was Carlos."

28

"Peter! Oh, what have I done?"

Chapter 5 The Man is Cain

In a small bookstore, they found three old magazines with stories about Carlos, bought them, and returned to the hotel. Minutes passed as they read, and then Marie sat up straight.

"It's here," she said, with fear in her face and her voice. "Listen. 'It is believed that Carlos and his soldiers commonly punish people by shooting them in the throat, leaving them to die in terrible pain. The punishment is for disloyalty or a refusal to give information.'" Marie stopped, unable to continue. "He refused to tell them about me and he was killed for it." She stared at Bourne. "But you knew about the gunshot in the throat. You *said* it!"

"I said it. I knew it. I don't know how. Am I one of Carlos's soldiers? Did I break the code of silence or loyalty? Is that how ..."

"Stop!" Marie shouted. "You are you. Don't take that away from me."

"Test me," Bourne said unhappily. "Take another of these magazine stories about Carlos and give me names from it. Let's see if I can tell you anything."

Marie looked at him, then picked up another magazine and looked through it. "Beirut," she said.

"Embassy," he answered. "CIA chief shot in the street. Three hundred thousand dollars."

Her voice shaking, Marie continued, "Novgorod."

"A Russian training school for spies. He spent time there."

"Tehran."

"Eight killings. Two million dollars."

"Paris," Marie said quickly.

"All contracts are agreed in Paris."

"What contracts? Whose contracts?"

"The contracts—killings. Carlos's."

"Carlos? Then they're *his* contracts, *his* killings. Not yours."

"But I knew—I know all this without reading the stories."

"What are you trying to tell me? You're Carlos?"

"God, no. Carlos wants to kill me, and I don't speak Russian. The only explanation is that I was with him and I left him. That's why I know too much about him to live."

Marie thought about it. "There's a problem with that," she said slowly. "Why haven't you just taken the money—all that money— and gone somewhere safe? Why don't we do that now?"

"Stop it!" Bourne cried. "I *can't* run. I have to *know*."

Marie took him in her arms. "I know. And I want to help you."

At the lawyer's office, arrangements for receiving the money went smoothly after Bourne increased the amounts that would be paid to both the lawyer and d'Amacourt. A messenger would carry the money from the bank in a leather case at 2:30 that afternoon and meet Bourne at 3:00 on a bridge over the River Seine.

"We understand," Marie told the lawyer finally, as Bourne's financial advisor, "that the special instructions with the account must be followed, but the timing must be to Monsieur Bourne's advantage. If not, I would have to report unacceptable activities that I have witnessed in the banking and legal professions here."

Back in the hotel, Bourne checked his gun while Marie phoned the Canadian embassy and spoke to Dennis Corbelier.

"That's strange," she said after their conversation. "He didn't know about Peter. He did find out about the telephone number that d'Amacourt gave you, though. It's a private line belonging to a fashion house called Les Classiques. It's a store, really, but all the clothes are designed by a man called René Bergeron."

By 2:15, Bourne was sitting in a taxi opposite the bank when a van drove out of the car park and parked in front of him. Fifteen minutes later, a man left the bank with a leather case and climbed into the van.

"Follow that truck," he told the taxi driver, "but keep two cars behind it." The driver looked worried. "I work for the

31

bank," Bourne explained. "I need to watch the truck."

When the van stopped in traffic, in a small street, he jumped out and ran to the van door, gun in hand. He shouted the code words through the door and ordered the van to stop.

"I've been told to meet you at the bridge, Monsieur!" the van driver said, opening his window slightly.

Bourne heard the low voice of a man in the passenger seat: "It *must* be at the bridge. We have orders." And then another man— the messenger?—"I want to keep my job. I'm getting out."

The messenger stepped out into the street, and Bourne threw himself against the door, knocking the second man back inside.

"Give me the money," Bourne shouted at the messenger.

"It's yours, sir. *They* wanted to find you. *I* meant no harm."

The van door crashed open again, and Bourne saw the face of Carlos's soldier, one of the killers from Zurich, and a gun staring into his eyes. He threw himself on the ground, turned, and fired twice. The killer fell. Bourne pulled the leather case full of money from the hand of the terrified messenger and ran.

Soon after passing the money to Marie and changing into more expensive-looking clothes, Bourne was at Les Classiques. It was a beautiful store on one of the best streets in Paris, employing beautiful women. Only a middle-aged man sitting in front of a switchboard at the bottom of carpeted stairs looked out of place there. Bourne walked around, admiring the clothes, until he saw her. It had to be her—a tall, cold-looking older woman who was walking down the stairs.

Immediately, Bourne started to play the part of a rich man choosing the most expensive clothes for his girlfriend. The woman looked interested and she waved the younger assistants away.

"You have good taste," she told him. "These are some of our designer's finest works."

"I'll take these three," he told her. "And maybe you could choose a few more similar ones. I've had a long flight from the

Oh, God! She was going with him!

Far away from Paris, in Washington D.C., a group of four high-level officials and a politician were also discussing Cain.

"Our information is that he was in Brussels, not Zurich, ten days ago," said an officer of the CIA. "A man was killed there, and the method was Cain's."

"But we have a report from Zurich," re-stated an army officer from the Pentagon. "Four men were killed there, including a man called Chernak. He is, without doubt, connected to Cain. Cain used him for payments for his kills."

"My worry is that too many recent assassinations are being blamed on Cain," said the third man. "What happened to *Carlos*, the most skilled assassin of our time?"

"We shouldn't forget him, but Carlos's time has passed." David Abbott belonged to the secretive Special Group of five men who were responsible for the country's relationships with foreign powers. "Cain is the new man. We must use all our informants, ask for the help of all European police forces, and catch him now. There have been too many killings. It has to stop."

The only politician in the room was looking confused. "I've been listening to you discussing an unbelievably dangerous professional assassin. My question to you is: Who is he? Who is this Cain?"

The silence lasted for seconds, while eyes found other eyes and saw agreement.

"He's a professional assassin, and his skills are for sale," the CIA man told him. "We can be certain of thirty-eight killings that he is responsible for, and twelve to thirteen more—many of them the deaths of other killers—are probable. For a few months recently, we thought that he, too, had been killed."

"But you don't know who he is?" the politician asked. "You have informants—they must know something."

"No two descriptions have been the same. We do know that he holds meetings at night, in dark rooms or streets. He speaks English and French—and Vietnamese."

"You know more." The politician moved forward in his chair. "You know where he came from."

"From South-east Asia. We believe, from Operation Medusa." The CIA officer pointed at an envelope on the desk. "These are the Medusa papers that might have information about Cain. Medusa was a very dangerous secret operation behind the enemy lines during the Vietnam war in the late 1960s. Teams of people—well-educated, but all a little crazy and often even criminal—destroyed enemy communications, looked for prisoners, and even assassinated village leaders who were working with the Communists. Most of them were killed, but some stole a lot of money from Medusa. Cain's codes and method of killing make us think that Cain is one of the men who worked for the United States on Operation Medusa in Vietnam."

"So his identity is in those papers?"

"Yes, but more than two hundred white males disappeared during Operation Medusa, and we don't know which one he is. We think he's American, but we don't even know that. Cain was working in South-east Asia until a year ago, when for some reason he moved to Europe."

"I wonder," said Abbott, "if he was jealous of Carlos. In my opinion he moved to Europe to show Carlos that he was better than him. If that's true, we should find Cain and then sit back and wait. When Carlos tries to kill him, we can take both of them."

The others agreed and the meeting soon ended.

While they were preparing to leave, Abbott pulled the Medusa papers toward him and looked quickly through the list of names. Where was it? He was the only one in the room who knew the name. Yes, it was there:

Bourne, Jason C.   *Last known position: Tam Quan*

Chapter 6 Messages

René Bergeron threw down the telephone on his desk. "We've tried every café, restaurant, and bar that she's ever been to!"

"And no hotel in Paris recognizes his name," said the switchboard operator. "It's been more than two hours now."

"She can't tell him much," Bergeron said. "She knows less than we do."

"She knows enough—she has called Parc Monceau, and she knows why."

"Tell me again—why are you so sure he's Bourne?"

"I don't know that. I said he's Cain."

"Bourne is Cain. We found him through the Medusa papers."

"Then he's Bourne, but he didn't use that name in Vietnam. Of course, many men had criminal records, so their identities were hidden. I know it's him. I was on an operation that he commanded, and I'll never forget it."

"Tell me."

"We went into an area called Tam Quan to save an American prisoner called Webb. On our way there, two members of the team disappeared—lost or killed, we thought. Then enemy gunfire surrounded us for two days and two nights. How did they know we were there? At night Cain went out alone to kill in the darkness, so we could move closer. I thought he was mad. On the third night we found the man, Webb, only just alive. We also found the two missing members of our team. They had been paid by the Vietnamese. Cain shot them in the head, then he got four of us and Webb—the others were killed—out of there. He was the coldest, most dangerous man I ever saw. Everyone was his enemy, even his own leaders, and he didn't care about either side in the war. But the pay was excellent, and there were many opportunities for us to make money."

"So he didn't use the name Bourne? What was his name?"

"We didn't use real names. To me, he was Delta."

"And then he became Cain … And now he wants to take Carlos's place. All over Europe, people know. He can be hired; contracts can be made; his price is lower than Carlos's. But we'll find him. *He* found *us*. And then Carlos will kill him."

♦

"I think we should talk about special instructions from Zurich," Bourne told Jacqueline Lavier as they sat in a restaurant twenty kilometers from Paris.

"My God …!" she cried. He had to hold her hand tightly to stop her leaving the table. "Why didn't I guess? Who are you?"

"My name isn't important," Bourne said, "but I'm not him. We're looking for him, too."

"Who is 'we'?"

"A company that wants its money. A lot of money. He has it."

"So he didn't earn it?"

"There's a disagreement," Bourne said carefully. "But why do you want him? Why is the telephone number of a Paris clothes store on special instructions in Zurich?"

"I am saying nothing," Jacqueline Lavier said. "Get out of Paris. You made the mistake."

"Mistake? *He* stole from *us*."

"Your *choice* was the mistake. You chose the wrong man."

"He took millions from us," Bourne said, "but you're not going to have it. I want you to stay away from him, all of you, or we'll pass information to the police about Zurich, the bank here in Paris, Les Classiques, everything—and start a big manhunt. We have friends in very important positions and we'll have the information first. We'll catch him."

"You won't. He'll disappear again! He's escaped once, twice, but we'll get him now. He won't escape a third time."

"We don't want you to have him. So stop your hunt tonight."

"You can't talk to me like that! Who do you think you are?"

Bourne paused, then attacked. "A group of people who don't much like your Carlos."

The Lavier woman's eyes opened wide. "You do know," she whispered. "And you think you can beat Carlos? You're mad. He has men everywhere. They will kill you in the street."

"You forget," Bourne reminded her, "that no one knows who I am. Only you, and you aren't going to tell anyone."

Madame Lavier's eyes showed her knowledge that she was now fighting for her life. "I can carry your message," she said. "What more do you want?"

"Why does Carlos want Bourne?"

The woman looked shocked. "*You* can ask *that*? He's Cain—you know that. He was your choice, your mistake." Cain. Bourne heard deafening thunder in his ears, felt pain in his head. The darkness was there again. Cain … Delta! "You insulted Carlos, and you are doing it again now."

Tell me. Tell me everything. At the end, there is only my beginning. I must know it.

"But why is Carlos so angry with Bourne? Pretend that I know nothing, and explain it to me."

"You paid the wrong … assassin. Because Cain has tried to take his place, Carlos will follow him to the ends of the earth and kill him. Let him have Cain and it is possible—only possible—that he might take your contract, the one that you gave to Cain. He has the contacts that Cain can never have—information that is *always* correct, from the highest places."

"That's Carlos," Bourne said, trying to control himself. "What else do you know about Cain? Where did he come from?"

"South-east Asia, of course. From the American Medusa …"
Medusa! The darkness, the sudden lights, the pain. Delta becomes Cain!
"Cain is American—we have a positive identification, bought in Washington. He has studied Carlos's methods and he copies

them. He is very skilled, a machine trained for Medusa. Before that, we know nothing. All records have been destroyed."

Bourne had one final question. "What happened in Marseilles?" he asked.

"Leland? The contract was accepted by Carlos."

"But many people think that Cain was responsible."

"Lies! The final insult. It was what Cain wanted people to think. He went there to do the job before Carlos could. Then it was said that he had been killed—taken from a city street to a fishing boat and later thrown into the water. Not true, of course. Now I need to use the ladies' room. You can stand outside the door."

Jacqueline Lavier was in the restroom for ten minutes before the pain in Bourne's head allowed him to notice. A light suddenly blinded him, and when he could see again a woman was standing in front of him with a camera in her hands.

"I met your girlfriend in the restroom," she said with a smile. "She asked me to give you this note." She walked quickly away.

… *You may be what you say you are, but you may not. The photo is on its way to Paris. If we have our agreement, that need not worry you. We will talk again.* …

He raced outside. "Taxi! Taxi!"

In the taxi, Bourne made a difficult decision. He would continue his search for his identity, but he would continue alone. He loved Marie too much to ask her to spend her life with an assassin. He would write her a note and find a way to disappear.

When he reached the hotel, he held her, running his fingers through her dark red hair. He lied to her about events at Les Classiques and said only that the store did seem to be an answering service and that he had arranged to meet the man at the switchboard later that night.

"Where did you leave the money?" he asked.

"At the Meurice Hotel. I took a room there."

"Let's collect it and then have some dinner."

As Marie used the bathroom, he wrote a quick note:

Go back to Canada and say nothing. I know where to find you.

He put the note on the table as they left the room. *I love you so much. But you cannot die with me. You must not. I am Cain.*

They collected the leather case and then stood in the street waiting for a taxi. Bourne looked at Marie. She was staring at something—in disbelief, in terror. Without warning, she screamed. He looked around, trying to find the reason, and then he saw the newspaper stand. He realized that he could not leave her now—not yet.

The front page of the newspaper read:

Woman hunted for Zurich killings

Suspect believed to have stolen millions

Under the words was a picture of Marie St. Jacques.

Bourne found some coins in his pocket, passed them to the newspaper-seller, took two papers, and pulled Marie away.

Back in the hotel, he poured Marie a drink. He heard her cry out, turned quickly, but was too late. She had the note in her hand.

"You were leaving! My God, you were *leaving* me!"

"Not now. *Listen* to me. I won't leave you now!"

"Why, Jason? Why?"

"Later. Just hold me. Let me hold you."

The minutes passed and Marie became calmer.

"Why did you do it?" she asked.

"To protect you. I'll explain. But first, let's talk about this." He pointed to the newspapers. As they read the story, Bourne saw the hand of Carlos behind it. Marie was a way of reaching Cain.

The report was in fact two stories. The first part placed the Canadian government employee at the scene of three murders. Fingerprints had, it said, been found and checked. The second part moved away from fact to fiction: Millions of dollars had, it was believed, been stolen by the Canadian woman and an American man from a secret numbered account at the Gemeinschaft Bank belonging to an American company called Treadstone Seventy-one. Bank codes had been broken using highly-skilled computer work and detailed knowledge of Swiss banking practices. A bank official, Herr Apfel, had agreed that a crime had been committed, but was unable to give any more information.

Marie let her copy of the newspaper drop to the floor.

"Lies," Bourne said. "Find you, and Carlos finds me. I'm sorry."

"But so much is true," Marie said. "The Gemeinschaft, Treadstone, Apfel. Swiss bankers don't talk. Apfel was ordered to talk, by someone very powerful. Why? Why was the bank made part of the story? This isn't one story—it's two. The second story was added to the first. Someone is trying to send us a message."

Chapter 7 Treadstone Seventy-one

It was a quiet street in a good area of Manhattan. No one would imagine that it contained one of the most secretive organizations in the United States. Only eight people in the country knew of its existence. Gordon Webb, now ringing the doorbell, was one of them, although he had never visited the house before.

Inside, he was welcomed by David Abbott and introduced to Elliot Stevens, a trusted assistant to the president.

"What did you find out in Zurich?" Abbott asked Webb when they were all seated.

"Carlos has men in Washington; maybe even in Treadstone. He found the special instructions and changed them. So he had already identified Bourne, the account-holder, as Cain ... That information is only in the Medusa papers."

"Good God! There are only three copies, and very few people are allowed to see them."

"One of those people is working for Carlos."

There was silence while the three men thought about this.

"I saw the newspaper report about the Canadian woman," Stevens said then. "Also Carlos's work?"

"Yes—we couldn't stop it, but she's not a killer. We simply added the equally false story about the missing money." He looked at Abbott. "Although that may not actually be false."

"But why did you use a Canadian citizen?" Stevens asked coldly. "The Canadians are already very angry about the death of one of their economists, who made the mistake of asking questions about an unlisted American company and was killed for it."

"We're trying to save her life," Webb said. "Bourne knows that the story's false. Through it, we're telling Bourne to come home."

"Jason Bourne," Abbott told Stevens, "is an American spy. There *is* no Cain in the sense that Carlos believes. He's a trap for Carlos. That's who he is. Or was."

"I think you should explain," Stevens said. "The President has to know."

"Three years ago we invented a man and gave him a life. He was a killer who raced around South-east Asia. When there was a killing, or an unexplained death, there was Cain. Informants were given his name. It appeared in embassy reports. Cain was everywhere. And he was. Bourne showed himself, always with a different appearance, speaking in one of a number of languages, talking to serious criminals as a professional criminal."

"He's been living this lie for *three years*?" Stevens asked.

"Yes. When he moved to Europe, he was known as the most skilled white assassin in Asia. There he saved four men who Carlos had been contracted to kill, and took responsibility for killings that Carlos had done. He has laughed at Carlos, trying to force him out into the open. I don't think there's any way a nation can repay a man like Bourne for the work he's done." Abbott paused. "If it *is* Bourne."

"What?"

"Too many things have happened that make no sense to us. He disappeared for six months, after he tried to stop Carlos's contract for the killing of Howard Leland. Then he came back. It was Bourne at the bank—the signatures were real. But who is he now? Who is he loyal to? Why is he with the woman? Why is she with him? Millions of dollars have been taken, men have been killed, and there have been traps for other men. But who for? Who *by*?" Abbott shook his head. "Who is the man out there?"

In a car further down the street, a European turned a switch. "That's all we needed to know," he said quietly to himself. "But you didn't tell them, Abbott, that on March 25, 1968, Jason Bourne was killed by another American in Tam Quan." He turned to the driver beside him. "Quick!" he said. "Get behind the steps to the front door."

The European took a long, thin gun with a silencer on it and followed the driver toward the house. The door opened. Stevens was being shown out. The driver fired twice, then both men ran into the building. In seconds, everyone in it was dead.

The European took all the paperwork he could find. It was more than he had hoped for—every code and method of communication used by the invented Cain. Then the final job. He picked up a glass and took a piece of tape from a small, plastic case in his pocket. He pressed the tape against the glass, then slowly took it off. He held the glass up to the light. The fingerprints on it were clear. He dropped the glass, took some of the pieces, and knocked others behind a curtain. They would be enough.

♦

Twenty-four hours later, four men met at a hotel in Washington D.C.; there was no time to look for a meeting place outside the city. These were the living members of Treadstone Seventy-one. Alexander Conklin worked for the CIA and, like one of

45

the two army officers, General Irwin Crawford, had been part of the Medusa operation. The fourth man was an old and much-admired senator from Colorado.

"I'm meeting the President tonight," the senator said. "Tell me everything you can. What happened?"

"Webb's driver found the bodies when Webb didn't return to the car," Crawford told him. "He wisely called the Pentagon, not the police, and spoke to me personally. I sent officers, but told them to do nothing until I arrived. I then called Conklin and we flew to New York with an FBI team. The place was completely clean except for a fingerprint on a piece of broken glass."

"Delta's," said the senator.

"Yes, and the glass was still wet with wine. Also, outside this room, Delta's the only person who knows about the house."

"It's unbelievable." The senator shook his head. "Why?"

"You know that he was never my choice," the general said. "In Medusa, Delta frequently disobeyed orders."

"He was usually right," said Conklin angrily. "You spent too much time in Saigon to know what was happening on operations."

"I'm just trying to show how his behavior could lead to the events on Seventy-first Street."

"I'm sorry," the CIA man said. "I know you are. Delta changed after his wife and children were killed in Phnom-Penh—it's why he went into Medusa and then was willing to become Cain. He hated that war, hated everyone in it. And I think you're right, Crawford. It's happened again. He went beyond his limits and became filled with hate. Look at the way he killed those men in Treadstone. We invented a man called Cain and now he *is* Cain."

"So why did he come back here?" the senator asked.

"I don't know," Conklin answered. "To kill us all? Does he know who the rest of us are? His only contact with us was Abbott. But I think we've become the enemy."

"And he knew Webb, of course," said Crawford. "But not through Treadstone."

"Yes, we shouldn't forget that. He even killed his own brother. We'll send his picture out now, to every contact, every informant we have. He'll spend money, he'll buy another identity. We'll find him. Then we have no choice—we have to kill him."

♦

They left the hotel quickly, but not quickly enough. Bourne saw the look of recognition on the receptionist's face as he paid the bill. The man's eyes were on Marie. As they ran for a taxi, he was reaching for the telephone.

Pretending to be American tourists, they asked the taxi driver to suggest a number of small hotels outside Paris. He drove them to one, and they immediately took a different taxi to another. By this time, Marie had changed her hairstyle and her make-up.

"So who do you think is sending us a message?" Bourne asked when they were in their room.

"I think they expect me to call the Canadian embassy, for their protection. Dennis Corbelier."

"No," Bourne said. "You're wrong." *It was sent by Carlos. I am Cain and you must leave me.* He saw the fear in her eyes. "All right," he agreed, "but do it my way."

He called the reception desk and asked for another room in the name of Briggs, for friends who would arrive later. Then he took some of his clothes, and hers, and arranged that room before he allowed her to call. She told Corbelier that she was innocent of the killings; that she needed help; that "he" was with her, and that they were using the name Briggs. Corbelier promised to send a car.

At two in the morning, they were standing outside their room in the darkness, listening, waiting, when the two men came. The men walked softly to Mr. and Mrs. Briggs's room, shot out the door lock with a silenced gun, and ran inside. More shooting followed before a light went on, then cries of anger.

When they had run out again, Bourne led Marie to the room and showed her what had been done to it, especially the bullet holes in the bedclothes.

"There's your message," Bourne said, as she cried in his arms. "And now I think you should listen to me."

But Marie had had another thought and was quickly on the phone, calling the embassy. As she feared, Dennis Corbelier had been shot in the throat at 1.40 that morning, on the embassy steps.

"I'll listen to you, Jason," Marie told him. "A message *was* sent, but not to us, not to me. Only to you."

For 1,500 francs, the receptionist was more than happy to lend his car. The guests were, he agreed, unlikely to find a taxi so early in the morning. Soon after that, Bourne and Marie were sitting in the small Renault in the middle of the countryside.

Three weeks before, in Switzerland, Bourne had started his story with the words: *My life began five months ago on a small island in the Mediterranean …* This time, he began: *I'm known as Cain.* He told it all—names, cities, dates … assassinations. Medusa. "We were wrong."

"Maybe," Marie said, "but also right. If that man existed, you're not him now. Can you walk away from it?"

"Yes," Bourne said, "but alone. I'm wanted by governments, and by the police. Men in Washington want to kill me because of what they think I know. An assassin wants to shoot me in the throat because of what I've done to him. In the end, one of those armies will find me, trap me, kill me. Do you want to be there?"

"No!" shouted Marie. "But don't forget—I'll die in a Swiss prison for things that I didn't do in Zurich."

"I can stop that. I could give myself to the police and take responsibility. I'm not sure how yet, but I will stop it."

"You see?" Marie said softly. "Is that what Cain would do?

Thank you for your offer, but I don't accept." She was quiet for a minute. "Jason, these two sides of you ... Is it possible that those crimes were committed but they weren't yours? That people want you to believe they're yours? Do you know how easy it is to make someone believe that they're someone else, through words and pictures, repeated again and again? Your memories could be false memories. It's possible that you've been used."

Bourne stared at her. "And if you're wrong?"

"Then leave me. Or kill me. I don't care."

"I love you ... I found two telephone numbers in Lavier's office. With luck, they can lead me to the number I need—to Treadstone. If I'm not Cain, someone at that number knows who I am."

Back in Paris, Marie called the Zurich number first— disconnected. From another phone, she called the local number.

"*La résidence du General Villiers. Bonjour?*★"

Marie stared at the phone, then put it down. "I've just reached the home of one of the most admired and powerful men in France."

Chapter 8 At Home with the General

"Villiers is a hero here," Marie said when they were back in their hotel room. "It's unbelievable to connect him with Carlos."

"But there is a connection. Is he still an army officer?"

"No, he went into politics. But he continues to argue for a strong France, with a strong army."

"Leland was assassinated because he tried to stop France buying and selling guns. There's the connection."

"But his son was killed—assassinated," Marie remembered. "*He* was a politician, too, and very popular. Surely his father

★ *La résidence du General Villiers. Bonjour?*: French for "General Villiers's home. Hello?"

49

wouldn't work with an assassin?"

"I'm going to talk to him," Bourne said. "If he doesn't know about Treadstone, he can find out. I'll tell him that the newspapers would be very interested in his relationship with Carlos."

A few hours later, Bourne was sitting in the Renault on a tree-lined street in the area of Parc Monceau when the old general came into view, leaving the house. Bourne stared at him. What madness had driven a powerful man like him into the terrible world of Carlos? As Villiers drove away, Bourne followed him.

After several hours in a country restaurant with other men of a similar age, all clearly army officers, Villiers left to drive home. Now was his opportunity. Bourne passed the general in the darkness, then turned suddenly and blocked the road. He opened his window and gave a cry.

He heard the old man climb out of his car and walk toward him.

"What has happened? Are you all right?" the general asked.

"Yes, but *you're* not," Bourne answered, holding up his gun. "Go back to your car and drive it off the road."

"*What?*" The old man stood up straighter. "Who are you? You will get nothing from me—and my family have orders not to pay terrorists. Use your gun, *garbage*, or get out of here."

Bourne stared at the old soldier, suddenly uncertain. "No one's ever doubted your bravery," he said. "But a general of France has become Carlos's tool ..."

The anger in Villiers's eyes was joined not by shock, as Bourne expected, but by hate. His hand shot up and hit Bourne across the face, hard.

"*Pig! Dirty pig!*" Villiers screamed. "*Garbage!*"

"I'll shoot," Bourne shouted, but he could not. He threw his gun out of the window and caught Villiers's arm. "Are you telling me you're not Carlos's man? Yes or no?"

Tears appeared in the old man's eyes. "Carlos killed my son," he said quietly. "That is why I left the army and went into politics."

They were soon sitting together in the front of Villiers's car.

"I'm being hunted by Carlos and I've discovered that your home telephone is being used," Bourne explained. "Someone is receiving and passing instructions. Do you answer the phone yourself?"

"Actually, I don't." The general was calmer now, but still shocked. "I have a private line. That number is answered by my cook or my driver, by my assistant or my wife."

"You'd better look closely at your employees."

"Impossible! I do not doubt their loyalty." He looked away. "An unnamed man traps me on a road at night, points a gun at me, says terrible things about me, and expects me to believe everything he says." He paused, then turned to Bourne. "And I *do* believe you—only because the anger in your eyes was real, and because you threw down your gun. Follow me back to Parc Monceau and we will talk more in my office."

"If someone recognizes me, I'm dead—and you are, too."

"It's late. Wait outside and I will call you if the house is quiet."

An hour later, Bourne parked the Renault in Villiers's street and looked across to the house. The old man was parked in front of him. Bourne noticed a light in the doorway, and then a figure on the step. Recognition followed—but a recognition that was beyond belief. *Was* this a trap? Had the old man lied?

He looked around but could see nothing else that was suspicious. No, it was not a trap. Something was happening that Villiers knew nothing about.

Two people were talking on the step: a youngish woman and a gray-haired man—the switchboard operator from Les Classiques. A face that brought back other memories, violent and painful. He heard explosions in his head, saw darkness, and had to look away.

When he looked again, the gray-haired man was walking down the street and the front door had closed. Bourne went

51

Was *this* a trap? Had the old man lied?

quietly to the general's car and knocked on the window.

"Who was that woman, on the step?" he asked.

"My wife," said the general in surprise. "My second wife."

"Your *wife*!" Bourne's shock was on his face. "I'm sorry," he whispered. "General, I can't go inside that house. The man with your wife … He's one of Carlos's contacts."

The blood left Villiers's face.

They drove to a park in another part of town. The old soldier knew that the younger man was not lying. It was in his eyes, in his voice. The old man wanted to cry. The man without a memory told him that he had to find Carlos, learn what the assassin knew; there would be no life for him if he did not. He said nothing about Marie St. Jacques, or the island in the Mediterranean, or a message sent through a newspaper report, or a hollow shell who could not be sure that his few memories were really his own. Instead, he told Villiers everything he knew about Carlos, while the general looked at him in surprise. Because of his son, the old man had seen the French government's secret papers on Carlos, and this stranger knew much, much more.

"My wife and I are often in different places," Villiers explained. "In many ways, we live separate lives. But I have always discussed my work with her—she is an intelligent woman, and I have found her opinions helpful. There could be a simple explanation for what we saw tonight—I hope there is, and I shall give her the opportunity to explain. But in my heart, I know there isn't." He looked sadly at Bourne. "Carlos does not only kill, and sell guns and bombs. He also sells countries' secrets. I and only five other men see all documents about our country's war plans. But regularly, we find that Moscow, Washington, or Beijing have this information. When I think back … She wanted the marriage, although she is so much younger. She has many interests that take her away, and sometimes I have wanted her with me but she has refused to come."

"Where was she last August?" Bourne asked.

"At home, and then in Marseilles, at a conference."

"On August 24 Howard Leland was assassinated in Marseilles."

"I know ... My *God!*" The old man's head fell. "She was with him. Carlos called her to him and she *obeyed*." He screamed in pain. Then he said, slowly, "I shall do what has to be done."

"You're going to kill her?"

"I will ask her to explain. If she tries to kill me, I will know— and then, yes, I shall kill her."

"Don't do it!" Bourne asked. "Hunt the killer, not his assistant. Help me—for your son. No one has ever been as close to him."

There was a silence, and then the old man spoke again. "You are right. So what can I do?"

"Carlos is looking for me, and he's near. Your telephone will become busier. I'll make sure of it. I'm going to talk to others at Les Classiques. Stay at home, pretend you're sick. Listen to phone conversations. Even if they realize you're listening, it will make their communications difficult. He'll need to have a meeting with your wife. Make sure that you know where she's going, and then call me on this number." He gave the number of his hotel room. "A woman will answer ..."

"A woman? You have said nothing about anyone else."

"There is no one else. Only her, and you can trust her. Carlos has tried to kill both of us. She didn't believe that you could be his."

"Then thank her for me. Now, begin your game."

Chapter 9 Trouble at Les Classiques

One telephone conversation with an assistant at Les Classiques was enough to give Marie all the names they needed. A satisfied customer, wanting to send gifts, could not be refused. A phone book then produced addresses.

Janine Dolbert was called at work and told to return home immediately. Bourne was outside her house, seized her by the arm, and walked with her.

"I work with a group of people," he told her, as she tried to shake herself free, "who are planning a trap for one of your customers—a killer. He's one of your most frequent customers, and we know that he's one of eight men. We've planned a trap, and we'll catch him in your store. Listen and watch. If you see me in the store again, tell me if you think you know who he is."

He left her in shock and traveled quickly to another part of town.

Claude Oréale was next to receive a message and to hurry home.

"We received a report from Zurich," Bourne said, "and we want you to tell Jacqueline Lavier." The man looked at him in disbelief. "Tell her that we can't trust the phones. Carlos is right."

"Carlos!" Oréale screamed. "What are you talking about?"

"They're planning a trap for him. He must stay away. Tell her."

Bourne left the shocked young man for his third meeting, knowing that he had started a wave of fear and confusion in Les Classiques.

◆

"Is this room 420?" said the voice on the line.

Villiers! "Yes," said Marie. "I know who you are."

"Tell our friend that my wife has been called to the phone six times in the last hour, and has now taken it into her room. I have picked up the phone a couple of times, then apologized for the interruption to her conversation, but she is, I think, becoming suspicious. I am beginning to sense violence in this house."

"Remember your aim," Marie told him. "Remember your son."

"There is more. One of the voices, a male voice, was odd— half-whisper, half-command. It changed quickly when they realized that I was listening, but I am sure. It was the *killer-pig*, and he was *instructing ... my ... wife!*" His voice broke with emotion.

"Please try to stay strong," Marie said. "It's very important that no connection is made between you and our friend. It could cost you your life."

"I think I have already lost it."

"*Vous êtes soldat! Arrêtez!**" Marie said sharply.

There was a silence. Then, "Thank you, my friend. You have reminded an old man of who he was—and must be again."

♦

It was dark when Bourne reached the apartment of Pierre Trignon, Les Classiques's accountant.

"I'm from the tax office," Bourne said. "I must instruct you not to leave Paris. My office will take your books when the store opens tomorrow."

"What?" Trignon was shocked. "There is nothing wrong with my books—nothing! What are you looking for?"

"Payments that were paid to companies that don't exist, and that were sent to a bank in Zurich."

"But every payment is signed by Madame Lavier. I just follow her orders."

"So who does she take orders from? Whose money was put into Les Classiques?"

"I don't know. Madame Lavier has many rich friends."

"Then it's possible that you and Madame Lavier are being used," Bourne said. "Money is going from the store to the Zurich account of an assassin called Carlos." Trignon screamed. "You should talk to Madame Lavier and start preparing your defense."

Bourne left. *Get Carlos. Trap Carlos. Find Treadstone. Find the meaning of a message. Find the sender. Find Jason Bourne.*

* *Vous êtes soldat! Arrêtez!*: French for "You are a soldier! Stop that!"

When he returned to the hotel, he learned from Marie that the calls to Parc Monceau had stopped, and that a woman matching Jacqueline Lavier's description had arrived at Villiers's house to speak to his wife. A gray Citroën was parked outside.

Bourne raced out of the hotel again, to Parc Monceau. There was no sign of the Citroën, but Villiers was standing on the doorstep.

"They left five minutes ago in a taxi," the general said. "My wife said that her friend wanted to see a priest at a church in Neuilly-sur-Seine. Two men followed them in the Citroën."

Bourne ran for a taxi and made his way to the church, arriving as Villiers's wife and Jacqueline Lavier were walking up the path. The Citroën was parked, but neither man got out. Bourne left his taxi and watched from across the street.

Minutes later, Villiers's wife hurried out of the church, carrying a white bag, and climbed into the back seat of the Citroën, which drove away. *A white bag!* Jacqueline Lavier's bag! Bourne started to move toward the church, then stopped. A trap? If Lavier was followed, he might be, too.

He looked around, but saw nothing suspicious, so continued toward the church. He stopped. A priest was coming out. Bourne had seen him before. Not in a forgotten past, but recently. Not as a priest, but as a man with a gun. Who? Where? As the killer turned right, the sun touched his face. Bourne froze. His skin was dark—dark by birth. He was looking at Ilich Ramirez Sanchez. Carlos.

Bourne took his gun from his pocket and ran toward him, pushing people out of the way, knocking against an old man. From his dirty clothes, the old man pulled a gun. Bourne threw himself into the street, over a car, as shots hit metal on each side of him. As screams came from people on the sidewalk, he raced through the traffic to the other side of the street. The old man disappeared into the crowd.

Where was he? Where was Carlos? Bourne saw him at the wheel

of a large, black car. He ran, but was too late. Carlos sped away.

Lavier! Now Bourne ran back to the church, and then inside. He looked around but could not see her.

"Excuse me, Father," he said to another priest, who was coming from a side room. "Two women came in a few minutes ago. Did you see them?"

"Yes, the younger woman helped the older one, who looked pale and sad, into that confession booth." He pointed. "A visiting priest is taking confessions today—although I thought I saw him leave."

"Thank you, Father. I'll wait for her."

Bourne waited until the priest had gone to the door of the church to see why ambulances were arriving outside. Then he went to the confession booth and pulled back the curtain. As he expected, Jacqueline Lavier was dead. Beside her was a fashionable bag—not hers—and in it was a note explaining why the poor, unhappy woman had decided to end her life. She asked for God's forgiveness.

He understood why Carlos had killed her—not for disloyalty, but for disobedience. Her crime was her visit to Parc Monceau.

Bourne decided that his next conversation should be with another messenger and a man, he was sure, from his past—Les Classiques's switchboard operator. Marie had learned that his name was Philippe d'Anjou. He found a payphone.

"D'Anjou?"

"Delta? I wondered when … Paris is not Tam Quan, Delta. We work for different employers now."

Delta! The name had been spoken. The name that meant nothing to him, but also everything. "Jacqueline Lavier is dead," Bourne said. "Carlos killed her half an hour ago."

"She's on a plane," d'Anjou replied, "with Bergeron."

"She's dead and you're next. Would she kill herself?"

"No."

"Call the church in Neuilly-sur-Seine."

Bourne ended the call and took a taxi to a different payphone. "D'Anjou?"

"So a woman killed herself. Who says it is really her?"

"It's her. I want to talk."

"No talking, Delta. But, in memory of Tam Quan—leave!"

"She went to Parc Monceau and she died for it. You've been there, too. He'll use you to trap me, and then he'll kill you." There was a long silence. "I only want information, and then I'll leave Paris. I'll see you in an hour outside the Louvre. There are men watching you. Tell them you're meeting me."

"You're mad! They'll kill you."

"Then you'll be well paid. An hour, d'Anjou!"

Before he left the payphone near Les Classiques, Bourne noted the men in a black car who were clearly watching d'Anjou. When d'Anjou left the store, his behavior showed that he knew they were there.

A taxi arrived and the black car followed. Bourne followed in another taxi. When he arrived at the Louvre, he saw the gray car that had followed Lavier and Villiers's wife to the church.

"Drive past that car. Three hundred francs," he ordered.

When they were beside it, he lifted his gun and fired at the back window. There were screams and the men threw themselves to the floor. They had seen him, though, as he had planned.

"Get out of here," Bourne shouted at the terrified driver, and as the taxi raced past the gates to the Louvre, he threw himself out.

He hid between two parked cars and watched the gray car following the speeding taxi.

The black car! He saw two men leaving the car and walking toward Philippe d'Anjou, who was standing on the steps. He ran until they were only a few meters from d'Anjou.

"Medusa!" he shouted.

D'Anjou's head came up in shock. The driver of the car

turned his gun on Bourne, while the other man's was pointing at d'Anjou. Bourne dived to one side and fired at the second man, hitting him. He moved to the left as shots passed him, and fired again. The driver screamed.

By this time men, women, and children were running in all directions. Bourne stood up. D'Anjou was hiding behind a great block of stone, and Bourne ran to him.

"Delta! It was Carlos's man. He was going to kill me!"

"I know. Let's go! Quickly!" Then he noticed, out of the corner of his eye, another, dark-skinned figure with a gun. He pushed d'Anjou down as four shots flew past them. *It was him!*

The pain returned to his head, the doors of his mind crashed open, then shut, as he ran after the man, then dived again as the man fired. Then Carlos raced away.

Minutes later, Bourne and d'Anjou sat in a back street café.

"I shall return to Asia," d'Anjou said. "I can't stay here."

"Tell me about Villiers's wife," Bourne said.

"Angélique? She is thought to be French, but she is Venezuelan. She is Carlos's cousin, and his lover—probably the only other person that he cares about. Villiers, of course, knows nothing."

"Now Treadstone. What do you know?"

"When I saw you, Delta, it seemed clear that you had made a very expensive agreement with the Americans. But what can *I* tell *you*?"

"Please. Just tell me what you—what *Carlos* knows."

"You became Cain, with a list of contracts that never existed, to make Carlos angry, bring him out, and catch him. Treadstone Seventy-one is the American government's most secretive group, formed by David Abbott, the same man who planned Medusa." Light and warmth were spreading into the dark corners of Bourne's mind. "I was told you were an American spy, but I knew you weren't—and that money wasn't the reason either. You are Cain for the same reason that you became Delta, whatever that is."

"Anything else?" asked Bourne urgently.

"Two things. First, the Americans think you are not working for them now—or they want Carlos to think that." *The silence— the message! They wanted him to return.* "Second, they know, of course, that your name isn't Jason Bourne."

"What?"

"March 25 is two days away. Carlos wants your corpse on that day—the day you killed Jason Bourne at Tam Quan."

Chapter 10 Friends or Enemies?

She opened the door to him and her large brown eyes moved around his face, afraid but questioning. She knew—not the answer, but that there *was* an answer.

"You were right," he whispered. "I'm not Cain because there *is* no Cain. He was invented to trap Carlos. I'm that invention. Delta, a man from Medusa, agreed to become a lie called Cain."

"But why?"

"There was a reason, but d'Anjou didn't know." Bourne told her everything that had happened, and what d'Anjou had said. As he spoke, he could see the happiness in her eyes.

" Jason!" she cried. "It's everything we felt."

"Not quite," he said. "I'm Jason to you, Bourne to me, because I know no other name. But it's not mine. They say I killed him in a place called Tam Quan."

"I'm sure there was a reason. And it's years ago. Now you must reach the men at Treadstone, because they're trying to find you."

"D'Anjou said that they think I'm not working for them now. What can I say to them? Will they believe that I lost my memory?"

"Contact Washburn. He'll have records of your illness."

"He's a drunk with a million dollars to spend. Even if he talks to them, how can the men at Treadstone be sure?"

But Bourne had no choice. He called the American embassy, identified himself as Delta, and asked them to contact Treadstone. Five hours later, he had followed instructions to call every hour but to stay away from the embassy, and he was becoming confused.

"They want me, but they're afraid of me," he said to Marie. "It doesn't make sense. When I'm inside the embassy gates, they'll control me. Instead, they don't want to touch me, but they don't want to lose me either. Let's get out of here."

When he called again, from another part of town, Bourne was told that a Treadstone officer had arrived from the U.S. and would meet him at a graveyard, the Cimetiére de Noblesse, south of Paris.

Bourne ended the call and stared at the phone. Another door was opening in his mind. He could see a gentle hill and white crosses. It was a place for the dead, but also for conversations. He saw a face, and then remembered a name: David Abbott. The man who was responsible for Medusa and for Cain. He shook his head.

"They've chosen a graveyard," he told Marie. "I've been there before, so I know the Treadstone man's real. If I don't come back, call Villiers. He's the only person we can trust."

He decided to take the Renault, which had been parked in an underground car park for some time now. As he walked in, he noticed a man drop down behind a car. The man didn't reappear. Who was he? How had Bourne been found? Of course—Carlos had found the receptionist who had lent them his car.

Bourne quickly lowered himself between two cars and moved on his hands and knees to a position behind the man. The man stood up slowly and looked around, confused. Then, realizing that there was a trap, he ran.

Now! Bourne jumped up and ran after him, knocking him to the floor. Then he pushed his fingers into the man's eyes.

"You have five seconds to tell me who's outside."

"A man—one man. In a car."

"You're Carlos's man, aren't you?"

"I don't know a Carlos. We call a number. I already called it."

Bourne pushed him to the Renault and into the driver's seat. The man drove him outside to the other car. Bourne pointed his gun at the second man and ordered him into the Renault, too.

Ten kilometers outside Paris, he let them out of the car in the middle of the countryside, but not before he had memorized the number that they had called.

Darkness came, and he was walking through the graves. Where inside this wide, fenced area would he be? Where did he expect Bourne to be? Rain fell, and a memory came to him of other, heavier rain. A brown envelope changing hands.

He suddenly noticed a faint light, moving from side to side among the graves. He wanted to call out, but he did not shout and he did not run. There was something strange about the movement of the light. Was the holder communicating with another man? He was. Someone was hiding behind a gravestone, and the light had caught the end of a gun. Bourne ran up behind him, seized the gun with one hand, and pulled the man's head back with the other, until it hit the gravestone and he fell unconscious. Bourne searched the man. He was not a government employee—this was a hired killer. Then Bourne ran around the graveyard and walked calmly toward the man from Treadstone from a different direction.

"My name's Conklin," the man said, "in case you've forgotten."

"One of many things," Bourne said. "I lost my memory and spent five months on a small island. A doctor there kept records."

"Of course he did. You paid him enough. We followed the money from Zurich—*our* money."

"I told you—I didn't know. Amnesia."

"But you found the money, and a woman to help you move

63

it. You killed Chernak, and three other men. And then you went to New York and shot them all: Abbott, Stevens, and Gordon Webb. We found your fingerprints. My God—your own brother!"

"What?" Pain shot through Bourne's head. *Fire. Explosions. Darkness.* When he opened his eyes, Conklin was pointing a gun at him.

"I promised myself I'd give you two minutes to explain yourself," the CIA man said. "We all lose people—it comes with the job. But who gave you the right to turn your gun against us?"

"You're wrong. It was Carlos—not me, Carlos! They know about the building on Seventy-first Street."

"Only eight people knew that address before last week. Three of them are dead, and we're two of the other five. If Carlos found it, you told him." Conklin's hand started to close on the gun.

"No!" screamed Bourne, and he turned quickly and brought his foot up to Conklin's arm.

As Conklin fell to the ground, Bourne saw another shadow appear behind a grave. He fired twice and the shadow fell.

Conklin was moving toward his gun. Bourne pointed his, but could not fire. He walked quickly away.

He returned to Paris.

"It was a trap," he told Marie. "I'm going to phone Villiers. His wife is our only hope. We have to make her talk." He picked up the phone and called. "General, we need to speak to your wife."

"I don't think so, Mr. Bourne—yes, I know your name now; my wife told me. I am afraid it won't be possible to speak to her. She saw the anger in my eyes. She saw that I knew. We talked and then she took my gun from beside the bed. I had emptied it, of course. So I put my hands around her throat and killed her. Now I will call the police and confess. Then I shall end my own life."

"No!" shouted Bourne. "You need *Carlos*—he killed your son. And *I* need him because without him I'm dead. Listen to

64

me, Villiers. Don't throw your life away. *You* didn't kill your wife—you must say that *I* did." There was silence on the other end of the line. "Your wife was Carlos's cousin and his lover. You can't punish her any more, but you can use her death."

"*Vous êtes soldat! Arrêtez!*" Villiers said, his voice shaking. "Someone reminded me recently that I am a soldier. What do you want me to do?"

"I'm going to send a note to Carlos, to make him even angrier. Then can you get me out of the country, to New York, with a false identity? I have a passport in the name of George Washburn. On the plane, I'll write down everything that's happened—that I know. I'll send it to you, and you can make the decisions if I don't return. And please protect Marie."

"I will. Why New York?"

"I have to prove that Carlos knew about a place where men were killed. He'll think I've killed his lover and he'll follow me to the end of the earth if necessary."

The man and the invention were finally one. There was no other way. He had to get Carlos.

Chapter 11 Rebirth

At 8:45 in the morning, the taxi moved slowly along Seventy-first Street. Bourne recognized everything. He thought of André Villiers. Bourne had written down everything that he could remember since his memory had begun to return, and had mailed the pages to Parc Monceau. The information would be used wisely and that knowledge gave him freedom. By the time it reached Paris, he or Carlos would be dead.

There was the house, and he had the feeling of *return*. He remembered a dark room—questions, endless questions: *Who is he? Quickly. You're too late. Where's this street? Who did you meet?*

Which of these killing methods do you use? No! Delta might do that, but not Cain. You are only what you have become here. He had written to Carlos that he was coming back here for the hidden documents that were his final protection. Now he understood what he had meant. His identity was inside that house. Whether Carlos came after him or not, he had to find it.

A moving van had stopped outside the house. Men climbed out and the front door was open. The house was being cleared! He had to reach Conklin. The men had to stop their work. The assassin would come at night.

The taxi driver spoke and Bourne bent forward to listen. As he did, a bullet raced past his ear and shot the driver in the head. Bourne jumped out and fell to the ground. Carlos was *here*, at the doors of Treadstone! He had brought him back. He ran to a café, asked for the phone, and called the CIA. He was told that Conklin was away. He was not expected back until the end of the week.

♦

The U.S. Secretary of State was a very angry man. He demanded from General Crawford an explanation of a long phone call from the American embassy in Paris.

A Canadian woman had arrived at the embassy, talking about Bourne, Delta, Medusa, Cain, Carlos, and Treadstone—about American lies to foreign governments and European newspapers without the knowledge of the Department of State. She said that a "friend," who was an important man in French politics, had suggested that this was the only way to save Bourne's life.

"I've listened to the tape of her story ten times and I believe her. He's an amnesiac," the Secretary explained to Crawford angrily. "A man who has tried for six months to find out who he is. We know he tried to tell you. And now he's bringing Carlos to us—unless you kill him first."

Crawford was silent. Could it be true? "Then the woman's our only hope," he said finally. "We know Cain's skilled at changing his appearance, but she may recognize him. I know where the action will happen, and it will be today."

"Fortunately for you, the woman's already here. We flew her over. But where—and why today?"

"At Treadstone—he wouldn't go anywhere else. And today, because it's the date of his own death."

When Crawford and Marie arrived in Seventy-first Street, they found that Conklin was already there. Marie sat in a government car a little way away from the Treadstone house, while the men went into a neighboring property.

"She's lying," Conklin said in the face of Crawford's anger.

"You're wrong, and you know it. He's here, and that proves it."

"Maybe, maybe." Conklin closed his eyes. "But it's too late. I hired gunmen to kill Cain and I can't stop them."

"Christ!" Crawford shouted. "At least send that moving company away."

"I've tried. I didn't bring it here." He picked up the phone. "Who signed the papers for removals at Seventy-first Street?" His face went white and he turned back to Crawford. "A man who left his job two weeks ago."

In the street below, Marie watched without recognition as a man in old clothes, carrying blankets, walked toward the house.

"I was told you needed more help," Bourne said to two moving men who were carrying boxes to the van. "I've brought blankets."

"Start at the top with the other new men," he was told.

Bourne climbed to the second floor. Which room? Memories returned. *Oh, God, it hurt!* He opened the door. Darkness, but not complete. A slight noise. He turned, terrified at the tricks being played in his mind. But it was not a trick! He saw the knife.

The hand! The skin! The dark eyes ... *Carlos!*

He moved his head back as the knife cut his chin. His foot

caught his attacker in the knee. Again the knife came toward him, but Bourne blocked the arm and pushed it up. The knife fell to the floor and Bourne reached for his gun. The metal toe of a shoe made contact with his head. He crashed into a wall, seizing his attacker's hand and breaking Carlos's wrist as he fell.

A scream filled the room, and then a bullet hit Bourne high in the chest. He jumped at the killer as more shots went wild. Then he heard the door crash shut and footsteps running to the hall.

Shots passed both ways through the door and then the footsteps ran downstairs. Shouts, and more gunfire. Carlos had organized the moving van! Some of the men in the house were his, but the assassin was killing the real moving men. In the distance, Bourne could hear the sound of the van speeding away. The front door was locked.

He was losing too much blood, but he knew that Carlos was also wounded. Jason Bourne had died once on this day. He would die again, but take Carlos with him. He went slowly down the stairs to the room where Cain was born.

Now. He pushed open the door and fired. Gunshots were returned. The *face*. He knew it. He had seen it before. It was known to many, he was sure. But from where?

A bullet hit him in the arm. Then the shots stopped and he could hear the sound of other men outside the door, the breaking of wood and metal, the men running into the building.

"He's in *here*!" screamed Carlos.

Why was the assassin calling attention to himself? But it had worked—the men were running past him. Carlos was escaping.

Bourne fell to the floor. "Carlos …!" he cried. He heard commands, then a man was walking toward him. A man who had tried to kill him in a Paris graveyard.

"You think you'll kill me—you won't!" Bourne said angrily.

"You don't understand." The voice was shaking. "It's Conklin, Delta," a voice said. "I was wrong."

He felt explosions in his head again, darkness, and then a clear memory. *Tam Quan. They had arrived. The prisoner was moving—he was alive. But a man was walking toward him with a gun. This man had trained with them, studied maps with them, flown with them—and told the enemy where to find them. It was Bourne. Jason Bourne. Delta fired at him.*

More darkness. Waves were carrying him into the night sky, then throwing him down again. He was entering endless, weightless ... memory. And then he heard the words, spoken from the clouds, filling the earth:

"Jason, my love. Take my hand. Hold it, Jason."

Peace came with unconsciousness.

◆

"What made you realize that he was in Treadstone?" General Crawford asked Marie.

"I didn't recognize him at first, but later it came to me: the man with the blankets! It was the way he held his head, to the right. But it's been almost two weeks now," Marie said impatiently. "Tell me! Jason—who is he?"

"His name is David Webb," Crawford told her. "Until five years ago he was a foreign services officer. His wife was Thai and they had two children. One day, while they were living in Phnom-Penh, a plane dropped two bombs on the area around his home and killed his family."

"Oh, God," said Marie quietly. "Whose plane was it?"

"It was never identified. Webb went to Saigon and trained for Operation Medusa. He became Delta, and he was very dangerous. The North Vietnamese couldn't kill him, so they caught his brother, Gordon, and held him. D'Anjou was one of the men who went with Webb to free him. Two of the others were in the pay of the North Vietnamese. One was Bourne, and Webb killed him. Years later, when Treadstone was formed,

Webb took his name."

"What was he doing when he was called to Treadstone?"

"Teaching in a small American college, leading a quiet life. Those are the most important facts, but there's one more detail that must be understood. He will now be protected twenty-four hours a day, wherever he goes, whatever identity he takes. He's the only person alive who has seen Carlos—*as* Carlos. He knows who he is—a public figure—but Carlos's identity is locked away in his mind. One day, he may remember."

♦

Marie went to the window and looked out. He was sitting quietly on the beach, facing away from the armed guards. The time here in the little house on the waterfront had been good to him. His body was whole again, and his dreams were less terrifying.

Suddenly, he jumped up and ran toward the house. Marie froze. Was the madness returning?

He rushed through the door, stared at her, and then spoke so softly that she could hardly hear him. But she did hear him.

"My name is David."

ACTIVITIES

Chapters 1–2

Before you read

1 Discuss what you know about Robert Ludlum and the story of
   The Bourne Identity. Then read the Introduction to this book.
   What have you learned from it that you did not already know?

2 Look at the Word List at the back of the book. Then explain
   how a person might feel—and why—if he or she:

   a suffers from amnesia
   b has nothing in his or her bank account
   c sees a corpse
   d has to confess a crime to the police
   e is a police informant
   f is trapped underground

While you read

3 Is this information about the patient true (✔) or false (✗)?

   a Someone has tried to kill him. .....
   b He speaks at least three languages. .....
   c He is probably a fisherman. .....
   d He has a bank account in Marseilles. .....
   e He is suffering from amnesia. .....
   f He has broken into buildings before. .....
   g He is used to driving expensive cars. .....
   h He has dangerous enemies. .....

4 Who:

   a recognizes the patient in Zurich? ....
   b learns that his name is Jason Bourne? ....
   c does Bourne send a gift of money to? ....
   d decides that he must go to Paris? ....
   e does Bourne use to help him leave the
     hotel? ....
   f passed money to the fat man for
     Bourne? ....

71

5 Discuss possible endings to these sentences.

    a The bank information was placed under Bourne's skin because …

    b Bourne is being hunted by …

    c He shouldn't trust the bank officials because …

    d If Bourne doesn't learn more about his past, he …

    e If Marie tries to run away again, he …

    f Next, he needs to go to …

Chapters 3–4

Before you read

6 Work with another student and have this conversation.

    Student A: Imagine that you are Marie. What has happened today? How are you feeling? What are you thinking? Tell Bourne.

    Student B: Imagine that you are Bourne. You are in a hurry to get to Löwenstrasse. Reply to Marie, but tell her as little as possible.

While you read

7 Write one word in each space.

    a What does Bourne learn in Löwenstrasse?

    Chernak was given the envelope of money for Bourne by a [1]........................ . Bourne took the money, so he [2]........................ the job. [3]........................ will pay anyone who kills Bourne.

    b What happens in Steppdeckstrasse?

    Bourne rents a [1]........................ and is visited by a [2]........................ . While he is resting, [3]........................ men come to kill him. As he leaves, two more men arrive with [4]........................ .

    c What happens in the gunmen's car?

    The men take Bourne's money and [1]........................ . He kills them and then goes to help Marie by the [2]........................ River.

    d What happens beside the river?

    Bourne [1]........................ Marie and [2]........................

her assassin. The assassin kills an [3]........................
man and escapes. Marie helps Bourne into the
[4]........................ .

e What happens in Lenzberg?
Marie finds a doctor for Bourne, but throws away
his [1]........................ . Bourne tells her his story and
tries, unsuccessfully, to make her [2]........................
him. She can help him in Paris because she knows
about [3]........................ organizations, and she works
for the Canadian [4]........................ .She phones
[5]........................, a friend, to ask him about Treadstone
Seventy-one. She tells Bourne that Carlos is a very
dangerous paid [6]........................ .

f What does Bourne learn in Paris?
At first, he believes that he assassinated the
American [1]........................, but then he realizes that he
was not in [2]........................ on that date. He learns that
special [3]........................ must be followed when he
tries to take money from his account. The bank official
has to call a number in [4]........................ . The phone
number will probably help Bourne to find
[5]........................ .

After you read

8 Discuss with another student what Marie asked Peter to do,
whether he succeeded, what happened to him, and why.

Chapters 5–6

Before you read

9 What kind of man is Bourne? Imagine that you are Marie, and
make two lists.

a Reasons why Bourne must be a professional assassin

b Reasons why Bourne can't be a professional assassin

While you read

10 Circle the correct words in these sentences.

a Carlos and his men often shoot people in the
heart / throat as a punishment.

b Bourne believes that he *is / used to work for* Carlos.

c When Bourne's account is active, a *bank / store* is called.

d Bourne finally gets his money with a *lot of / little* difficulty.

e In Madame Lavier's office, Bourne finds and memorizes telephone numbers in Zurich and *New York / Paris*.

f The man at the switchboard has known Bourne by the name of *Briggs / Cain*.

g A CIA officer tells others in Washington that Cain is a *CIA informant / professional killer.*

h During the Vietnam war, Cain worked for the *Americans / Vietnamese.*

i David Abbott says that *Carlos / Cain and Carlos* must be killed.

11 Write the names.

  a the designer at Les Classiques   ....

  b the documents identifying Bourne as Cain   ....

  c the American saved in Tam Quan   ....

  d the name that Bourne was known by then   ....

  e the assassin who takes Carlos's contracts   ....

  f the assassin who killed Ambassador Leland ....

  g the person wanted by the Zurich police   ....

  h the Zurich banker named in the report   ....

After you read

12 Have this imaginary conversation.

  Student A: You are Bourne. You have learned where Dr. Washburn is now. Telephone him and tell him how you are feeling and why.

  Student B: You are Dr. Washburn. Ask Bourne questions and help him understand what is happening to him. Thank him for the money and tell him what you are doing now.

Chapters 7–8

Before you read

13 Chapter 7 is called "Treadstone Seventy-one". What are you going to learn about Treadstone, do you think? Discuss which statements might be correct.

a It is a secret organization.
b It is part of the United States government.
c It employs Carlos.
d It used to employ Bourne.
e It knows about Bourne's time with Dr. Washburn.
f It does not trust Bourne now.

While you read

14 Who or what is described by the words in *italics*?

a "*He* found the special instructions and
changed them." ....

b "There are only *three copies* ..." ....

c "We're trying to save *her* life." ....

d "*He's* a trap for Carlos. That's who *he* is.
Or was." ....

e *He* held the glass up to the light. ....

f "*He* even killed *his* own brother." ....

15 Complete these sentences.

a Marie thinks she is being contacted by
....

b Bourne thinks the message is from
....

c But he allows Marie to call
....

d Gunmen attack the room that is in the name of
....

e At about the same time, Corbelier is shot in the
....

f Marie realizes that Bourne's memories could be
....

g The Paris number from Les Classiques belongs to a
....

h Villiers hates Carlos, who killed his
....

i Outside Villiers's house Bourne sees, again,
....

j Carlos's contact inside Villiers's house is
....

After you read

16 Discuss these statements about Bourne. What have you learned about his past?

    a "On March 25, 1968, Jason Bourne was killed by another American in Tam Quan."

    b "He hated that war, hated everyone in it."

    c "Three years ago we invented a man and gave him a life."

    d "He even killed his own brother."

Chapters 9–10

Before you read

17 Discuss these questions.

    a Can Bourne trust Villiers, do you think? Why (not)? Is there anyone else that he can really trust?

    b What is Bourne going to do next? What will the effect be?

While you read

18 Who:

    a frightens Janine Dolbert and Claude Oréale? ....

    b becomes suspicious of General Villiers? ....

    c reminds the general to stay strong? ....

    d is told that Les Classiques pays an assassin? ....

    e visits Parc Monceau? ....

    f leaves a church in the clothes of a priest? ....

    g is found dead in the church? ....

    h does Bourne save outside the Louvre? ....

    i is Carlos's cousin? ....

    j contacts the American embassy? ....

    k tries to have Bourne killed at a graveyard? ....

    l kills General Villiers's wife? ....

    m *pretends* that he killed her? ....

After you read

19 Work with another student. Imagine and practice one of these conversations. Then act out the conversation to the rest of the class.

    a Pierre Trignon and Madame Lavier after Bourne's conversation with Trignon

b Jacqueline Lavier and Angélique Villiers at Parc Monceau

c Philippe d'Anjou and his contact, on the telephone, after Bourne's first call to him

d Bourne and an official at the American embassy, when Bourne calls for the first time to identify himself

e General Villiers's conversation with his wife before her death

Chapter 11

Before you read

20 Think about Bourne's plan now.

a What do you think it is? What is his aim? What could go wrong? Will he succeed? Make notes.

b Use your notes to give a two-minute talk to another student about Bourne's plan. Listen to his or her talk. What do you disagree about?

While you read

21 Write short answers to these questions.

a Who has Bourne sent all his memories to?

....

b Who and what does he expect to find inside Treadstone?

....

c What is happening to the Treadstone building?

....

d Why isn't Bourne killed in the taxi?

....

e How has the U.S. Secretary of State heard Bourne's story?

....

f Why will Marie be useful at Treadstone today?

....

g What does Bourne pretend to be doing as he enters the building?

....

h Who is waiting for Bourne on the second floor?

....

22 Correct these sentences. Cross out the wrong word and write the correct one.

    a First, Carlos attacks Bourne with a gun. ....

    b Bourne breaks Carlos's leg. ....

    c Then Carlos is shot in the chest. ....

    d Some of the men in the house work for a moving company; others work for Conklin. ....

    e Delta died on this day, years before. ....

    f Bourne is shot again, in the head. ....

    g When men enter the building, Carlos dies. ....

    h Conklin takes Bourne's hand as he becomes unconscious. ....

After you read

23 Give this information about Bourne's true identity.

    a What is his real name?

    b What happened to his wife and children?

    c What was his job before their deaths?

    d What was his job after their deaths?

    e Where did he work after that?

    f When did he start using the name of Bourne?

24 What do these sentences mean? How is this recognition important to Bourne's future?

    The face. *He knew it. He had seen it before. It was known to many, he was sure.*

25 Is there anything about the story that you haven't understood? Write down any questions. Then ask other students to explain it to you.

Writing

26 Write Dr. Washburn's notes on his patient's problems and treatment. How was Bourne when he left his care?

27 Choose one of the pictures in this book. Explain why this is an important time in the story.

28 Write Bourne's note to Carlos (Chapter 10) to make sure that he will be at the Treadstone building in New York.

29 Write a page in Carlos's secret diary about the events in New York on March 25.

30 Write a report from General Crawford to the U.S. President about the aims and methods, failings and successes of Treadstone.

31 Write a conversation between Bourne (now David Webb) and Marie later on the day when the story ends. Start:
DAVID: I've never really understood. Why have you stayed with me all this time?

32 A year after the story ends, what is Marie doing and how does she feel now about the events of a year ago? Write a letter from her to a close friend in Canada.

33 Imagine and write about the life of a character in this book who is less important or who does not appear at all.

34 Explain which actors you would like to play three of the main characters in a new movie of this book, and why. (Matt Damon is busy with other work.)

35 Describe two important events in your own past—one that you would be happy to forget and one that you would like to remember forever.

Answers for the activities in the book are available from the Penguin Readers website. A free Activity Worksheet is also available from the website. Activity Worksheets are part of the Penguin Teacher Support Programme, which also includes Progress Tests and Graded Reader Guidelines. For more information, please visit:
www.penguinreaders.com.

WORD LIST

ambassador (n) the most important official who works for his or her country in another country. The country's **embassy** is the building that the ambassador works in..

amnesia (n) a medical condition in which you lose your memory. An **amnesiac** is a person who has lost his or her memory.

assassin (n) a person who murders, or **assassinates**, someone, usually for political or financial reasons

(bank) account (n) an arrangement that allows you to keep your money in a bank and take it out when you need it. An **accountant** keeps and checks financial records for a business.

code (n) a system of using words or numbers instead of ordinary writing so that a message can only be understood by someone who knows the system; the rules that govern a person's behavior

conference (n) a large, formal meeting of a lot of people, often lasting several days

confess (v) to tell people that you have done something wrong or illegal. A **confession booth** is a place in a Catholic church where you confess because you want God to forgive you.

contract (n/v) a formal agreement between two or more people, stating what each person will do

corpse (n) the dead body of a person

design (v) to do a drawing or a plan of how something will be made

general (n) an officer with a very high position in an army

grave (n) a place in the ground where a dead body is put

identity (n) who you are. If you **identify** someone, you recognize and correctly name them.

informant (n) someone who secretly gives information about other people, often regularly

instruct (v) to tell someone what to do

lawyer (n) someone who gives advice about the law and may speak for people in court

obedience (n) the act of obeying a person or rule

priest (n) a church official, with duties and responsibilities in a church